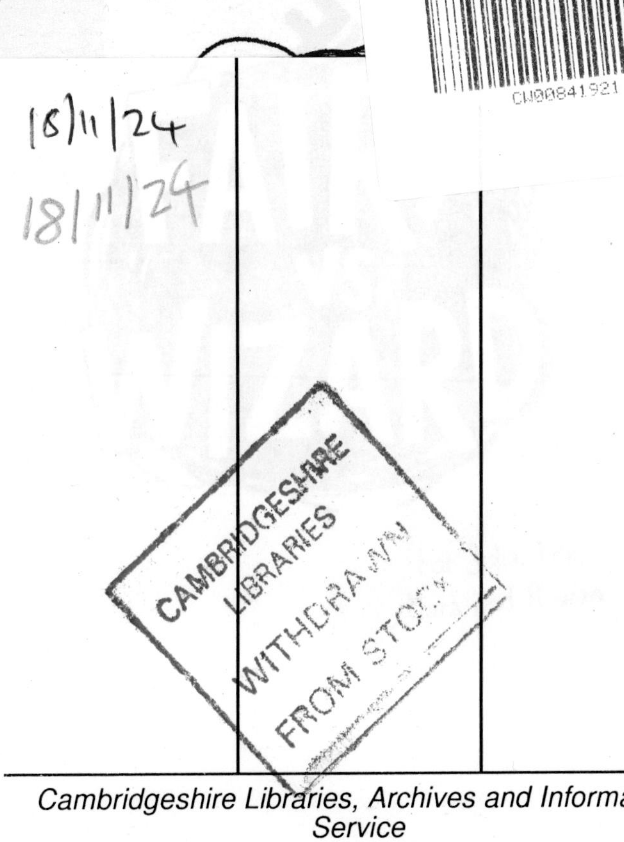

Cambridgeshire Libraries, Archives and Information Service

This book is due for return on or before the latest date shown above, but may be renewed up to three times unless it has been requested by another customer.

Books can be renewed –
in person at your local library

Online www.cambridgeshire.gov.uk/library

Please note that charges are made on overdue books.

CAMBRIDGESHIRE LIBRARIES	
10010010721369	
Askews & Holts	04-Mar-2024
JF	

N… …, Ireland

Text and illustration copyright © Jenny McLachlan 2024

The moral rights of the author and illustrator have been asserted

ISBN 978 0 00 852430 2

Printed and bound in the UK using 100% renewable electricity at
CPI Group (UK) Ltd

1

A CIP catalogue record for this title is available from the British Library.

All rights reserved. No part of this publication may be reproduced, stored in a retrieval system, or transmitted, in any form or by any means, electronic, mechanical, photocopying, recording or otherwise, without the prior permission of the publisher and copyright owner.

Stay safe online. Any website addresses listed in this book are correct at the time of going to print. However, Farshore is not responsible for content hosted by third parties. Please be aware that online content can be subject to change and websites can contain content that is unsuitable for children. We advise that all children are supervised when using the internet.

This book contains FSC™ certified paper and other controlled sources to ensure responsible forest management.

For more information visit: www.harpercollins.co.uk/green

WORDS AND PICTURES BY

JENNY MCLACHLAN

1. FAIRY VS WIZARD

Some stuff you need to know . . .

1. My name is Danny Todd
2. I'm eleven years old
3. I've just started at a new school called MOS Academy*
4. I've got two rats called Tony and Noah
5. I've got a fairy called Stink

On the next page I've drawn a comic to explain how I ended up with my own fairy.

TONY

*Our school is actually called Mumbles-on-Sea Academy, but everyone calls it MOS Academy for short. That's MOS to rhyme with moss, the soft green stuff.

HOW I ENDED UP WITH A FAIRY BY ME, DANNY TODD
On my birthday my little sister, Sophie, gave me a fairy door.
Without my permission she stuck it to my bedroom wall.
To get revenge I told her I could make a fairy come out of the door and said this stupid rhyme . . .
Oh FAIRY, OH FAIRY, OH FAIRY WHO EATS JAM . . .
AND A FAIRY DID COME OUT!
F.A.R.T.

She said . . .

My name is S.Tink*.
I work for the Fairy Assistance Response Team.
Every time I help a human do a good deed I earn 100 gold nuggets.

F.A.R.T.
ALES AUXILIUM

(Like this but loads more.)

Then she said . . .

You're my boy, Danny Todd, and I'm not going to leave you alone unless you help me do a good deed so I can get new wings.
RUBBISH WINGS

*S.Tink won't tell me her first name so I call her Stink.

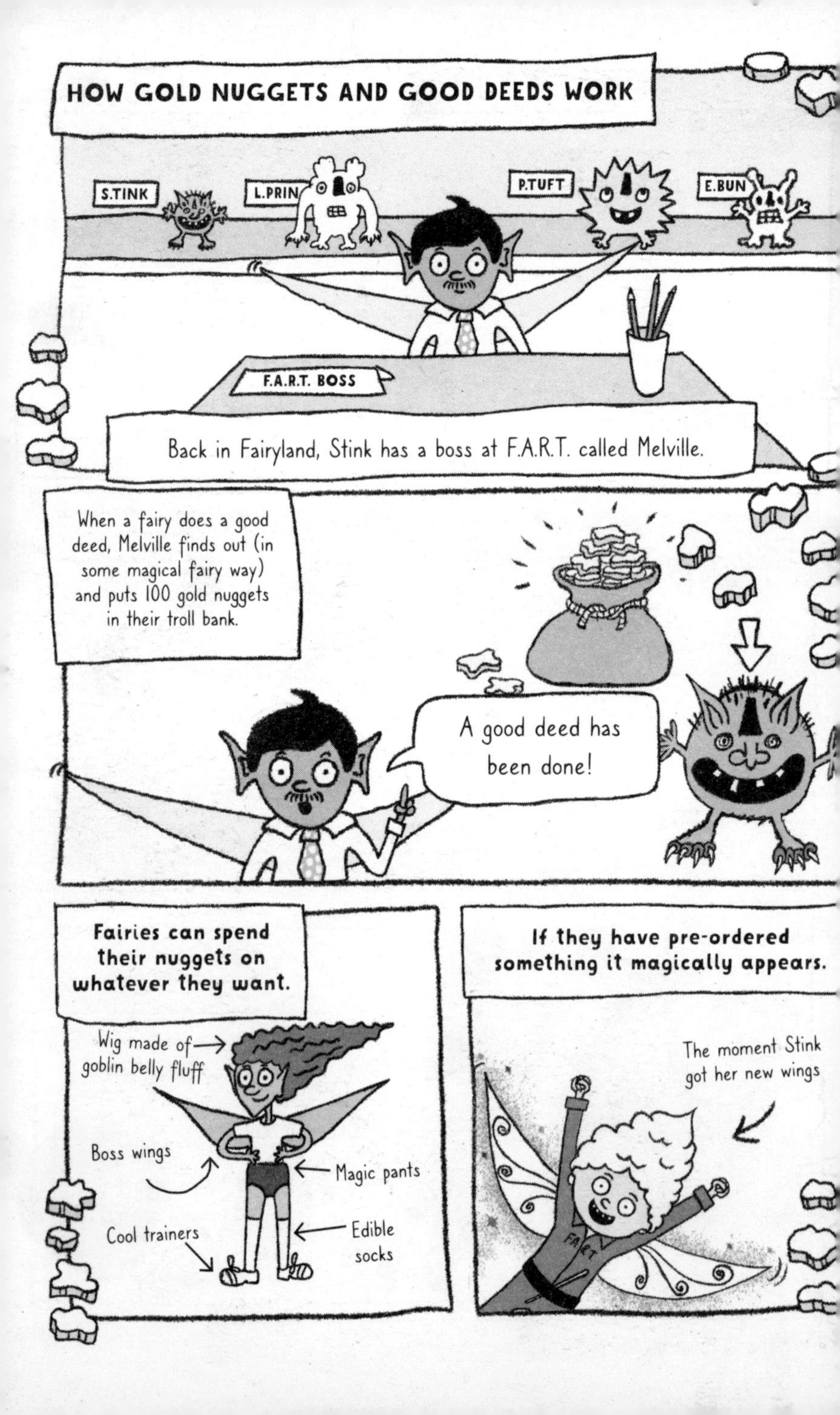
HOW GOLD NUGGETS AND GOOD DEEDS WORK
S.TINK
L.PRIN
P.TUFT
E.BUN
F.A.R.T. BOSS
Back in Fairyland, Stink has a boss at F.A.R.T. called Melville.
When a fairy does a good deed, Melville finds out (in some magical fairy way) and puts 100 gold nuggets in their troll bank.
A good deed has been done!
Fairies can spend their nuggets on whatever they want.
Wig made of goblin belly fluff
Boss wings
Magic pants
Cool trainers
Edible socks
If they have pre-ordered something it magically appears.
The moment Stink got her new wings
FART

As I helped Stink do a good deed I found out she could do spells like . . .
STICKING SPELL!
RED!
GLUE
SHRINKING SPELL!
YELLOW!
EXPLODING SPELL!
GREEN SEVENTEEN!
OFF-WHITE!
COLOUR-CHANGING SPELL!
To make the spells easy to remember Stink has given them the names of colours.

'OLLEY!
To undo a spell, Stink says the colour backwards.

The only people who found out about Stink were my best mate, Kabir, and my sister, Sophie.

FART
With our help Stink earned her 100 nuggets, got new wings and went back to Fairyland.

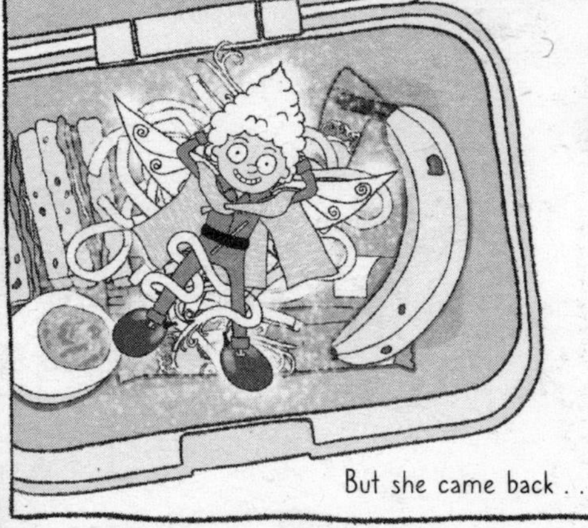
But she came back . . .

2.
MY EGGY FAIRY

So yesterday I found Stink in my lunchbox and she couldn't have chosen a **WORSE** time to come back into my life. I want everyone at my new school to think I'm cool and funny, but so far that hasn't happened.

For one thing, Mum is making me wear pointy shoes that make me look like a business elf.

Plus, Dad put boiled eggs in my lunchbox even though I told him not to.

And then I found Stink.

I was so shocked to see her, I made a big mistake. I **SPOKE** to her.

Everyone started giving me funny looks so I slammed the lid shut and pretended I was talking to a grape. Too late I realised that talking to a grape was even stranger than talking to a lunchbox, especially as I did a special voice for the grape.

I made Stink stay in my lunchbox for the rest of the day and only let her out when we got home. She'd got a bit messy in there.

Once I'd picked all the egg off her wings, we had this conversation . . .

Stink, why have you come back through the fairy door? You **PROMISED** you would go back to Fairyland and leave me alone for ever!

Yeah, well, I lied. Sorry about that, Danny.

You don't look sorry.

I'm sorry **INSIDE** where you can't see it. Don't worry. I've just come to Humanyworld for a minibreak. I'll go home tomorrow.

So I agreed to let her stay, then I gave her some ice cream and we watched a Muppets movie.

That was yesterday. I'm going to school now and Stink has promised she'll be gone by the time I get home.

3. TOUGH FAIRIES

Stink **DID** go back to Fairyland, but only for a bit. When I got in from school I found her sitting on my bedside table, crying. Straight away I noticed that her posh wings had gone and her tatty ones were back.

Then she told me what had happened.

MY SAD STORY By S.TINK

I was **fl**ying down Dragon Alley when a gang of tough fairies jumped on me and stole my cool new wings.

But that wasn't all. My brother, Fandango, saw it happen and didn't do **ANYTHING** to help! He just laughed and said . . .

'You are so pathetic S████*. You are an embarrassment to the Tink family and fairies in general. If you knew awesome magic like **ME** then you could have put a jelly jinx on those fairies!'

*Stink **STILL** won't tell me what her name is!

But I could **NEVER** have done a jelly jinx because my wand is rubbish! Anyway, Fandango tossed his hair (that's actually a wig made out of mermaid hairs) over his shoulder, and said, 'See you later, loser!' and shot off using his Zeus 223 wings.

'So you see I had to come back,' said Stink.

'Because you need to do a good deed so you can get new wings?' I replied

Stink looked at me like I was stupid and said . . .

No way! I'm over wings now. I want a **NEW WAND**. Mine sucks. Sometimes it works and sometimes it doesn't. I can't do any good spells with it.

Then she showed me this leaflet.

Kabir's right, Stink. Stay in my hair, keep quiet and keep your wand in your pocket.

Oh, don't worry, Danny. I'm going to stay in your hair. There are loads of grown-ups at school and I can't let them see me. You know what happens if a grown-up sees a fairy. We melt and turn into magic goo that can burn through ANYTHING!

I'm not sure if this burning-magic-goo-thing is true, but seeing as Stink spends a lot of time in my hair the thought of her melting makes me feel nervous. Obviously I don't **WANT** her in my hair at all. This morning I told her to get into my rucksack, but she refused and said that because I trapped her in my lunchbox she's now scared of the dark.

Stink broke her no-talking rule the second we walked into our form room. Our teacher, Miss Nichol, asked me and Kabir to hand out some textbooks. When Stink saw Miss Nichol she cried out, **'SOOOOOO PRETTY!'**

Miss Nichol froze, clutching her mug of tea. Then she said, 'What did you just say to me, Danny Todd?'

I went bright red. I suppose Miss Nichol is quite pretty, but I would never in a **BILLION YEARS** tell her this. Kabir came to my rescue.

Pretty is slang, Miss. It means wicked. Danny was just saying those, er, chemistry textbooks look totally wicked. Right, Danny?

I love chemistry. Look at those test tubes on the front cover . . . like, **WOW!**

Great – I mean, **pretty.**
I guess that means you'll be joining my after-school chemistry club, Danny? It's massively **pretty.**

Um, yes, please.

Then I handed out the textbooks.

Stink broke Rule Number Two seconds later when she shot out of my hair and flew into Miss Nichol's cupboard. A few minutes later she flew out and asked if she could stay there for the whole day. She said it was messy and tidying it up might be her good deed.

I agreed because not having Stink hanging around with me all day sounded like a great idea, but I made her promise to stay in the cupboard.

After school, Kabir and I sneaked back into our form room to pick up Stink. She hadn't done any tidying up, but she had made a fairy playground out of Maltesers and science equipment.

Can you imagine my horses playing on this?

Just so you know, Stink hasn't really got horses. She's got five **FOXES**, but she thinks they're horses because she learned all about Humanyland (our world) from a dodgy textbook. She also thinks my rats are baby dragons, worms are snakes and woodlice are chocolate croissants.

Anyway, last time Stink visited she shrank down some foxes using her YELLOW spell and I let her take them back to Fairyland.

Apparently they're having a great time there. They've grown back to their normal size and they give lifts to old fairies who are too tired to fly.

One of the foxes, Rosy, lives with Stink in her tree hole.

By the way, I'm writing this in my neighbour Professor Najin's tree house. Stink and Kabir are here too. Helping Professor Najin was Stink's last good deed and it's how Kabir and I ended up being mates with an old lady. Najin doesn't know about Stink which is a shame because I think they'd get on. They're both wild and grumpy and enjoy lazing around and watching telly.

Anyway, we love spending time at Professor Najin's because she lets us do whatever we like. For example, she's let us turn her tree house into a **MIND-BLOWING** den. See for yourself.

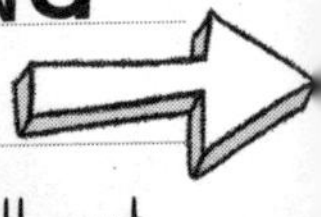

Stink has her own chill-out area with a hot tub that's made from a chicken tikka masala carton. Kabir and I make the bubbles by blowing through a straw.

Hang on, Kabir wants to write something:

*He isn't and I didn't.

5. CHEESE SNEEZE

My dad made macaroni cheese for dinner tonight. Sophie got told off for putting two pasta tubes up her nose then 'sneezing' cheese sauce out, and Stink hasn't done any good deeds.

All she did at school today was:

- Eat Miss Nichol's lipstick
- Add a zip wire to her fairy playground
- Burp during French and get me told off

I got a break from Stink after lunch when Kabir took her to PE. She was supposed to stay in the pocket of his shorts during football, but she fell out when the whistle blew and got stuck to the ball. She said it was amazing until she fell off and got trodden on.

6.

THE GOLDEN-BALL-THINGY

Except for Stink and Sophie painting our dog, Frida, on Jas's bedroom wall with nail varnish, not much happened over the weekend.

Today, however, Stink did one **GOOD** deed and one **BAD** deed.

I'll tell you about the good deed first. While Mr Harvey, our history teacher, was telling us about Henry VIII, Stink removed all the old chewing gum stuck under my desk. I thought she might be about to earn her nuggets until she started eating the chewing gum and got it stuck in her hair.

I spent break time cutting it out.

The BAD deed happened at lunchtime when I went to the canteen with Kabir and our new friends, Mara Thompson and Cooper Cole. As soon as I opened my lunchbox Stink whispered, 'I'm hungry.' Then she noticed Mara's Scotch egg.

Obviously I didn't reply, but Stink would not shut up about the Scotch egg.

'Tell me what that golden-ball-thingy is,' she said, her voice getting louder. 'Tell me, Danny. **TELL ME!**'

'A Scotch egg,' I whispered as quietly as possible.

Mara gave me a funny look. I smiled at her.

BUT WHAT EVEN IS A SCOTCH EGG?

Did you say something, Danny?

No.

I bent down and pretended to tie up my shoelace. I hissed, 'Shut up, Stink. You're not allowed to talk, remember?'

She said nothing, but I could feel her wriggling around in my hair and I guessed that she was hiding herself away. Good, I thought, but when I sat up, Mara, Cooper and Kabir were all staring at me.

'What's the matter?' I said.

'There's a Scotch egg in your hair, mate,' said Kabir.

'IT'S MY SCOTCH EGG!' cried Mara.

I tried to get it back, but Stink wouldn't let go and we ended up having a tug of war over the Scotch egg.

When I finally got it back, Mara didn't want to eat it.

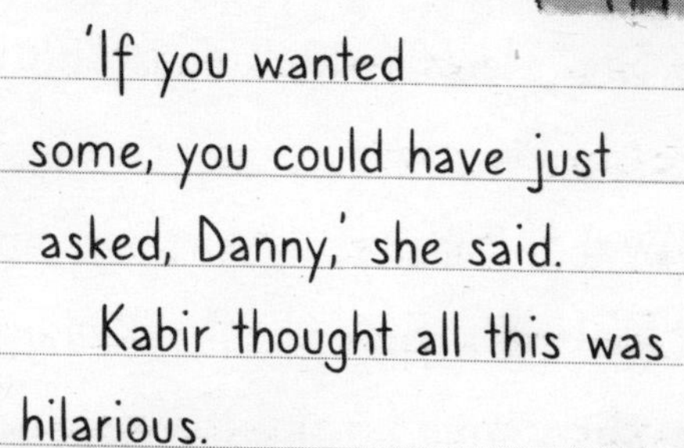

'If you wanted some, you could have just asked, Danny,' she said.

Kabir thought all this was hilarious.

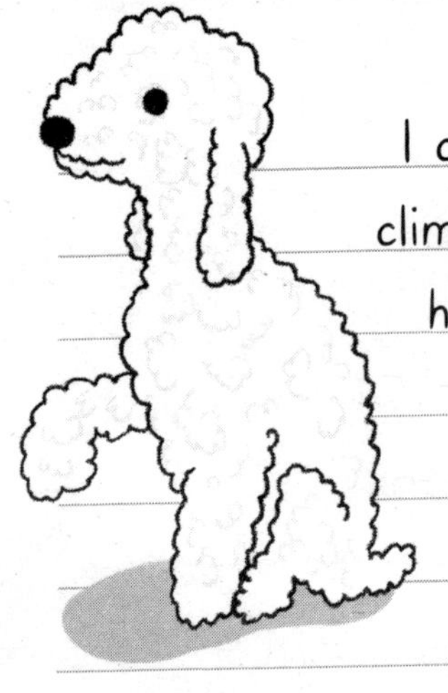

I couldn't believe it. Mara goes climbing and can do tricks on her mountain bike. Cooper got to the finals of a Lego competition and has a dog called Lamb Dog that looks like a lamb.

They are nice and funny and I want to be friends with them, but that's never going to happen now because they think I'm the sort of boy who steals Scotch eggs and tries to hide them in his hair!

All that happened hours ago and Stink thinks I'm making a fuss about nothing. As I write this she's lying on my fluffy pencil case and being groomed by Tony.

7.

TUESDAY

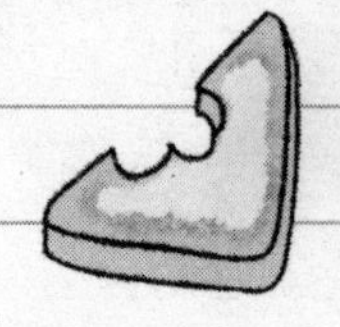

Good news! Stink isn't coming to school with me today. My sister, Sophie, has a cold so Stink has decided to stay at home and 'look after her'. She says she might earn nuggets for it, but I know that really she just wants to watch Disney films.

UPDATE: surprise, surprise, Stink didn't earn any nuggets, but she did watch *Tangled*, *Frozen*, *Frozen II* and *Brave*.

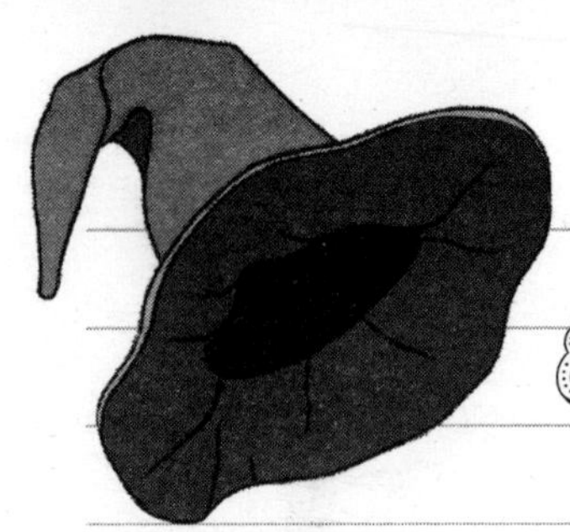

8. 7N'S EPIC ASSEMBLY

I've had two more Stink-free days at school because Stink caught Sophie's cold. This means school has been very relaxing and today we got some exciting news.

Our form group – 7N – is going to do an assembly and Miss Nichol has written us a play called:

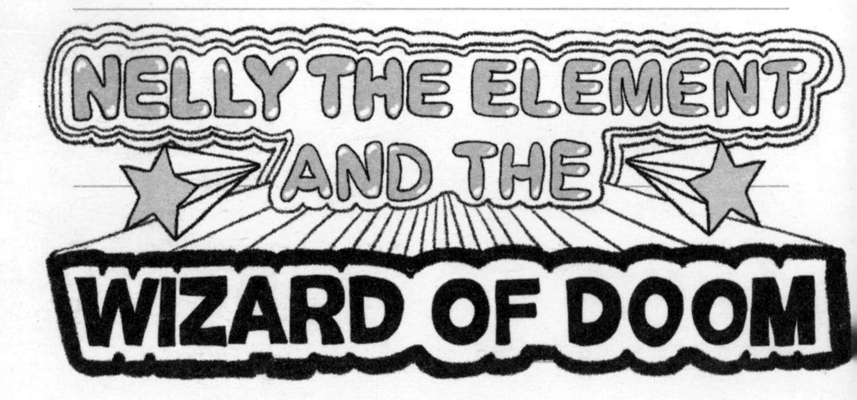

Miss Nichol says the play is about being a good friend, but we all know that really she's trying to teach us about science because Nelly the Element has a gang of friends called things like Zara Zink and Humza Helium.

She's made this cast list . . .

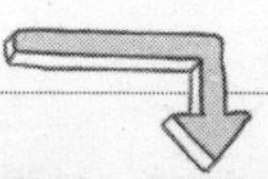

NELLY THE ELEMENT AND THE WIZARD OF DOOM

An original production written and directed by Sarah Nichol

The Wizard of Doom wants to steal Nelly the Element's golden petri dish, but Nelly has a secret weapon: her friends. Together Nelly and her friends will teach the Wizard of Doom that the greatest power of all isn't his formidable magic, but their fab friendship!

Nelly the Element: a kind, fun girl who loves chemistry

Nelly's gang: Zara Zink, Humza Helium, Ian Iron, Sancho Silver

(Nelly's gang are great at teamwork, dancing and rapping)

The Wizard of Doom: an all-powerful, all-terrifying magic man

The Wizard of Doom's gang: Mingus Meanalot, Sam Snide, Martha Mockysocks

Miss Nichol is really excited about the play. As she sipped her cup of coffee, she told us that at the weekends she does something called Live Action Role Play, or LARP for short . . .

I'm a LARPer. At the weekends I meet up with my LARPer friends and we dress as fantasy characters and have adventures in the woods. Well, mainly we have battles. It's loads of fun. I'm usually an elf queen called Zandra and my boyfriend, Scott, is a viking-ninja-demon called Drath.

Then she showed us some photos of her dressed up as Zandra.

I'm going to use my LARP skills to make 7N some amazing costumes and I'm going to show you how to do realistic pretend fighting. Oh, and we're going to have **REAL** magic! My brother works at Trix-4-All Magic Shop and he says he can get me a discount. The Wizard of Doom is going to have fire coming out of his fingers and a smoking cloak. 7N's assembly is going to be EPIC!

Miss Nichol is **THE BEST** form teacher. Of course, everyone wants to be the Wizard of Doom and have flaming fingers.

After Miss Nichol had told us this, Fin Budgen (who also lives next door to Professor Najin) said that **HE** should be the Wizard of Doom because he's the tallest in the class and can do the splits. Then his twin sister, Poppy, said that **SHE** should be the Wizard of Doom because she can do the splits **AND** backflips.

Anyway. Got to go. Stink has got stuck in an apple and Kabir is rolling her around.

9. FRIDAY MORNING SURPRISE

Something strange has happened. I was just getting dressed for school when the fairy door flew open and Stink came out carrying a bulging bag. She must have gone back to Fairyland during the night.

What's in the bag?

Just some F.A.R.T. equipment like ropes and stuff. I'm supposed to bring it with me on all my missions to Humanyland, but it's heavy so I leave it in my tree hole. It's time for me to do my good deed.

I'm pleased that Stink's taking her good deeding seriously. We're off to school now and she's bringing her bag of equipment. If she earns her 100 nuggets today then I might be fairy-free by this evening. Tomorrow Kabir and I could take Najin's SUP board out on the river and I won't have a fairy to worry about. Happy days!

10. BIG NEWS

Friday evening update: I regret ever letting Stink come to school with me. I regret it from the bottom of my heart.

She has ruined my life.

Here's what happened.

BAD FAIRY!
Turn the page to find out why . . .

During form time, Stink shot out of my hair and disappeared into Miss Nichol's cupboard. She's always doing this so I didn't think anything of it, but a few minutes later a ginger

snout poked out of the door. I blinked. I wasn't imagining it. The snout was still there. There was **A FULL-SIZED FOX** in Miss Nichol's cupboard!

Suddenly another snout appeared followed by a bushy tail and then three more snouts. There were **FIVE FOXES** in Miss Nichol's cupboard!

I sat there, desperately hoping no one would see them. The second Miss Nichol finished the register and everyone went to assembly, I sneaked into the cupboard.

This is what I saw . . .

Hello, Danny!

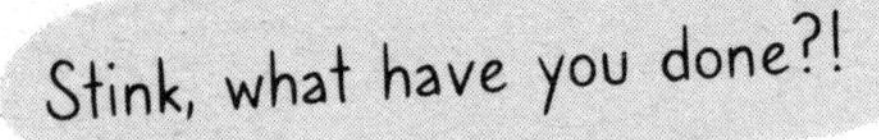

Stink, what have you done?!

I wanted my horses to have a go on my playground so last night I went back to Fairyland, shrank them down, then smuggled them here in my F.A.R.T. bag.

So your bag isn't full of special equipment?

No. I can't believe you fell for that, Danny!

Why are the foxes so big?

Because the spell has worn off and they've grown back to their normal size.

Just then we heard footsteps. Someone was coming!

Do the **YELLOW** shrinking spell again, Stink! Miss Nichol **CAN'T** find me and five foxes in her cupboard. I'll get in so much trouble!

They're horses, Danny, and I was just about to shrink them – they can't go on the slide when they're that big, can they?

Then Stink got out her wand and shouted, '**YELLOW! YELLOW! YELLOW! YELLOW! YELLOW!**'

For a moment nothing happened, then her wand made a strange fizzing sound, a couple of stars burst out and the five foxes shrank down until they were the size of beetles.

IT'S A MATCH!

Just then a voice behind me said, 'Danny Todd, what are you doing in my cupboard?'

I turned round and saw this . . .

'I got lost,' I said, trying to block Miss Nichol's view of Stink's Malteser playground.

She narrowed her eyes and said, 'Hmmm . . .' followed by, 'Hurry up or we'll be late for assembly.'

As I left the cupboard I felt Stink fluttering into the back of my hair. Lucky escape, I thought.

11. DISCO DANNY

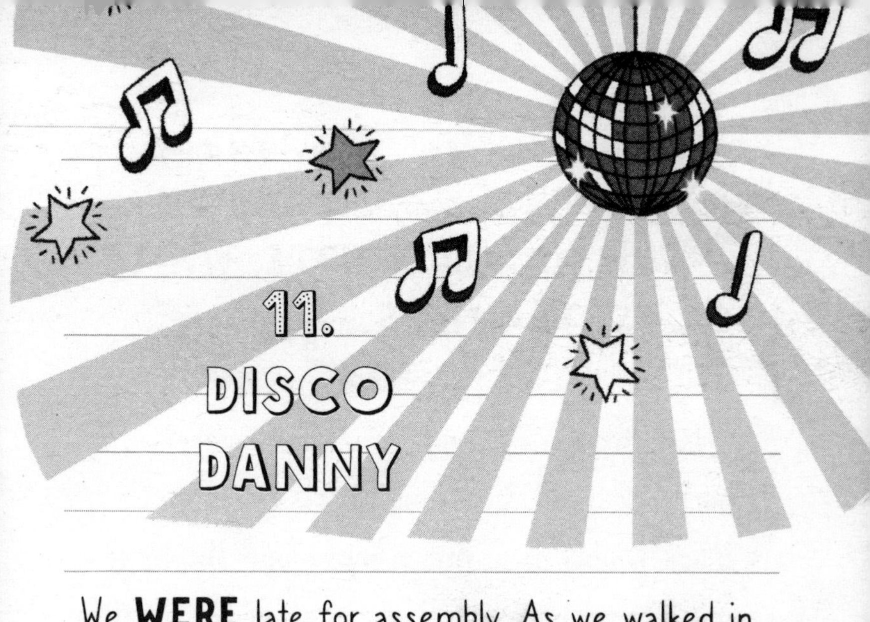

We **WERE** late for assembly. As we walked in our head teacher, Mrs Busby, was in the middle of giving everyone a lecture on uniform.

Mrs Busby said, 'Year 7s, you have only just joined MOS Academy and already I'm seeing **UNTUCKED SHIRTS, WHITE SOCKS, TRAINERS** and . . . ah . . .'

Her beady eyes fell on me.

'Now there's a young man who is very smartly dressed. Come up here!'

Miss Nichol gave me a shove and the next thing I knew I was standing next to Mrs Busby on the stage.

What's your name?

Danny Todd.

'Well, Danny Todd, you look very smart. Look at the shine on those pointy shoes! Year 7s, take a good long look at Danny Todd.'

Mrs Busby put her hand on my shoulder. 'Here is a boy who has followed the uniform expectations to the letter. Doesn't he look fine?'

I'm now going to show you a short film about our uniform expectations at MOS Academy and I'm going to ask Danny Todd to remain where he is as an example to you all.

It was terrible. Mrs Busby had just told **EVERYONE** in my year that I was a nerd who always followed the rules. I mean, I **AM** a nerd who always follows the rules, but I don't want this advertised.

Suddenly dance music echoed round the hall and the video began to play.

I kept as still as possible and hoped Stink would too as I waited for the film to end. But it was long. MOS Academy has so many uniform expectations!

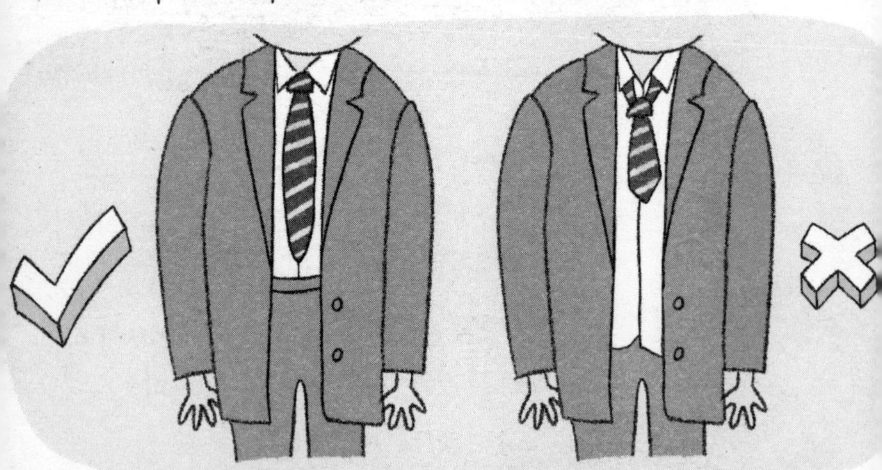

As a series of banned items of uniform flashed on the screen, I heard Stink say, 'Uh-oh!' and then tiny feet began to trot over my scalp. It was so tickly!

I desperately wanted to scratch my hair, but I kept my hands shoved in my pockets. Next I felt the tiny feet go skittering down my neck and the back of my shirt. Stink hissed in my ear, 'The horses have escaped, Danny!'

The foxes went burrowing under my clothes and gambolling all over my body. One shot into my armpit and started snuffling around. Another went down my trouser leg then back up the other side. I felt a snout digging around my tummy button. I managed to handle being tickled, sniffed and nibbled by the tiny foxes, but as the music got louder, and

NO TRAINERS

. . . started to flash up on the screen, I lost it.

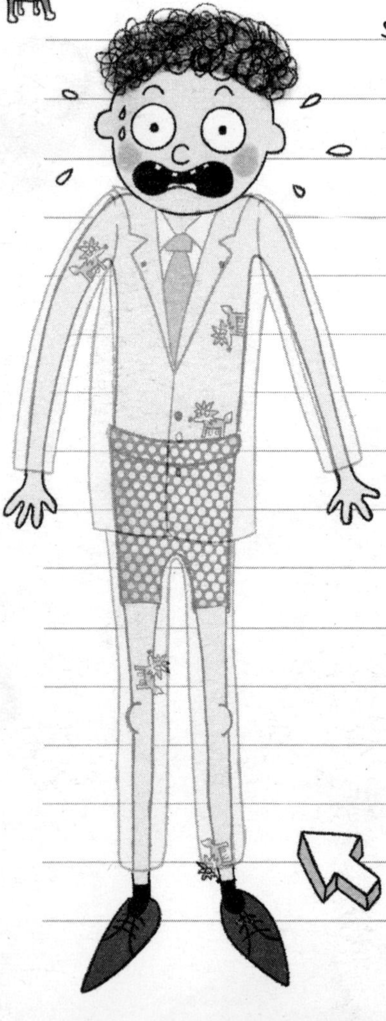

=Fox

I have made my clothes see-through so you can see what the foxes were up to

AND
THIS IS
WHAT
I DID.

As the video finished, I managed to shake all the foxes out of my trousers and they scurried behind a curtain. When I looked up, I saw this . . .

12. DISCO DANNY CONTINUED . . .

Because I had 'played the fool' and ruined her assembly, Mrs Busby gave me an after-school detention. But that wasn't all. For the rest of the day, whenever I saw another Year 7 student they shouted 'Disco Danny!' and started imitating my dance.

OI, DISCO DANNY!

Even Stink was cross because I'd lost her precious horses (foxes) and she had to spend the rest of the day rounding them up.

As we walked out of school (well, I walked, Stink sat in my blazer pocket) Stink tried to cheer me up.

Don't worry, Danny. I found all the foxes and I promise I'll send them through the fairy door as soon as we get back to your bedroom.

That didn't make me feel much better. I've only been at MOS Academy for a few weeks, but already I've got a bad nickname and **EVERYONE** is laughing at me. I even saw two teachers doing the Disco Danny dance in the car park.

I bumped into Miss Nichol by the gates.

Just then three Year Ten girls at the bus stop started doing the Disco Danny dance. One of them was my sister, Jas.

Miss Nichol watched them for a while, then said . . .

Listen, Danny, when something like this happens you've got to wait for it to blow over.

Then my phone beeped. Kabir had sent me a message.

Someone filmed your dance and turned you into a GIF mate!

Then I saw a wobbly video of me on the stage dancing. The word **LOSER!** flashed at the bottom of the screen.

'I don't think it will blow over, Miss Nichol,' I said, and I showed her the Disco Danny GIF.

She pulled a sad face and said, 'Hang in there, Danny. I promise everyone will be talking about something else on Monday.'

Three more students shouted 'Disco Danny' at me on the way home and Kabir kept sending me updates about my GIF. When he told me it was the forty-sixth most popular 'What a loser' GIF on Giphy, I turned off my phone and hid in my bedroom.

Stink sent the foxes back to Fairyland and while I've been writing this she's been playing on my finger skateboard. She's made a halfpipe out of a melon and two books. She's getting quite good.

13.

BARDZO SZARPANY TANIEC

Because it's Saturday I thought I might get a day off from people laughing at me, but Jas shared the Disco Danny GIF with the family WhatsApp group and this is what happened at breakfast.

After breakfast my grandma in Poland rang me up to tell me she'd sent my 'bardzo szarpany taniec*' to all seventeen of my Polish cousins and they were all 'śmiali się do rozpuku**'.

After this, Stink flew into my hair and we went to meet Kabir. Our plan was to buy sweets then spend the whole day at Najin's. We were halfway to the shops when we bumped into Cooper Cole. He told us that my Disco Danny dance was going viral on TikTok.

*Very jerky dance

**Laughing their heads off

I tried not to look at the comments, but they leaped out at me.

Imagine!?! 

he is SOOOO bad

Suddenly I didn't want to go and buy sweets. What if I saw someone from school and they started doing the dance? I glanced around. I was surrounded by people looking at their phones. Any one of them could be looking at the Disco Danny GIF!

So I said to Kabir . . .

I just remembered that I'm supposed to be doing something?
What could be more important than eating sweets with me?

I pretended not to hear and left him with Cooper.

The day only got worse. Stink let Tony and Noah escape and they ate Mum's secret supply of Haribo. Mum was so cross that she made me play dressing up with Sophie and I've been forced to spend the afternoon pretending to be a 'skeleton princess'.

Now I'm sulking in my room watching Stink practise her ollies.

Worst. Day. Ever. (Except. For. Yesterday.)

14. SUNDAY

Today I hid at home and Stink kept me company. I didn't turn my phone on once, but that didn't mean I was free from Disco Danny because Jas did the dance every time she went past my bedroom door.

I DO NOT want to go to school tomorrow.

15. DANNY THE WIZARD

When I walked into our form room today I found Poppy and Fin Budgen teaching Miss Nichol a familiar dance.

'Miss Nichol, you said everyone would have forgotten about the Disco Danny dance by today, but you're learning it!' I said.

She must have felt bad because after she'd taken the register she called me up to her desk.

I've had an amazing idea. I've thought of something that will make **EVERYONE** forget about Disco Danny.

Then she thrust this MOS Academy newsletter under my nose.

DEMY
TTER
MBLY TIME!
ike to invite family
friends of M.O.S
cademy to their
erformance of . . .
LY THE ELEMENT AND THE
WIZARD OF DOOM

I'm going to make **YOU** the Wizard of Doom in 7N's assembly! Do it well and you won't be **DISCO DANNY** any more. You'll be **DANNY THE WIZARD!**

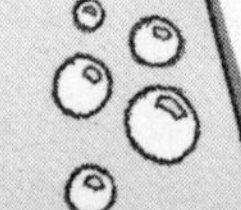

I swallowed. I wasn't sure I was ready to get on that stage again or if being Danny the Wizard was better than being Disco Danny, but Miss Nichol had made up her mind. 'I'll type up the cast list now,' she said.

Kabir and Stink weren't sure about her plan either.

FART
YOU'RE going to be the Wizard of Doom?

But Miss Nichol said the Wizard of Doom was an all-powerful all-terrifying magic man. That's not really you, is it mate?

I agreed with Kabir, but Miss Nichol was already pinning the cast list on the noticeboard.

Mara is Nelly the Element and Kabir and Cooper are in her gang.

The rest of 7N were surprised to see that I was the Wizard of Doom, but they were all nice about it. Except for Fin and Poppy.

DANNY TODD?!?
IS THIS A JOKE, MISS NICHOL?

Being cast as the Wizard of Doom made me forget about Disco Danny for a bit, but as soon as I walked to my next lesson, I caught glimpses of the film on phones everywhere. And kids kept staring at me and whispering.

Kabir said that they were probably staring at **HIM** because he's put a new video on his YouTube channel of him unboxing a pair of trainers, but I know he was just saying this to make me feel better.

All day I've tried to imagine me stepping on to the stage with fire leaping from my fingers and terrifying the audience . . .

. . . but I can't see it happening.

This evening I told Stink that I wasn't sure if I should be the Wizard of Doom.

She said, 'Yeah, I know what you mean. It might make things worse. Your trousers could fall down.'

This wasn't what I meant, and now I'm worried about that as well.

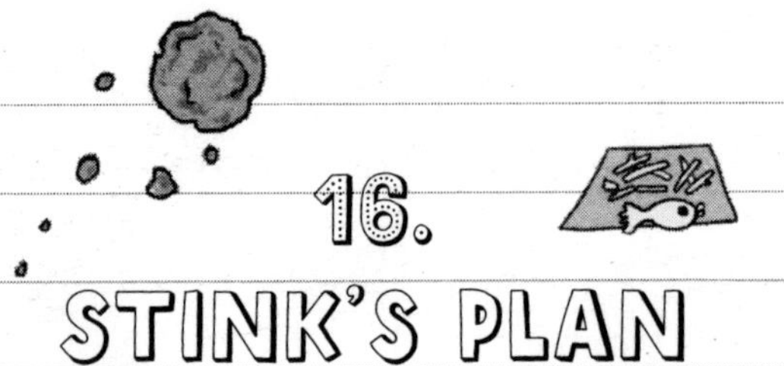

16. STINK'S PLAN

Stink woke me this morning by lifting up one of my eyelids with her wand and shouting . . .

'What's the matter, Stink?' I said.

I know what my good deed is going to be . . . I'm going to make sure you're an **AMAZING** Wizard of Doom!

How can you do that?

You're not going to believe this, Danny, but when I was at school my best friend was a wizard called Rufus Nobeard. I bet if I went back to Fairyland and asked Rufus to come and give you wizarding lessons, he'd do it.

There's no way you are bringing anything else through that fairy door.

You need him, Danny. Imagine having your own **REAL-LIFE** wizard to train you up. He can teach you to do wizard magic.

But then Stink went and ruined everything by telling me a bit more about Rufus Nobeard*.

Rufus was the smallest wizard in school and he literally had no beard and EVERY wizard has a beard, Danny, even baby ones. Plus, he didn't stride about like other wizards.

A NORMAL WIZARD BABY

He scuttled and his voice was quiet like a whisper. Also, he didn't hang out with the other wizards doing powerful magic. He was shy so he played Humanyland with me.

Humanyland was our favourite game. We would pretend to eat fishes and chips and drive cars and play football with a ball

made out of gnome dung.

Rufus Nobeard was a great mate, but I've not seen him since I got chucked out of school for blowing it up. I've often wondered how he got on without me. I was his only friend.

I told Stink that a small, shy wizard couldn't help me be an amazing Wizard of Doom, but she just smiled and said . . .

*Stink wrote this and helped with the pictures because, as she says, I don't know anything about Fairyland or Rufus Nobeard.

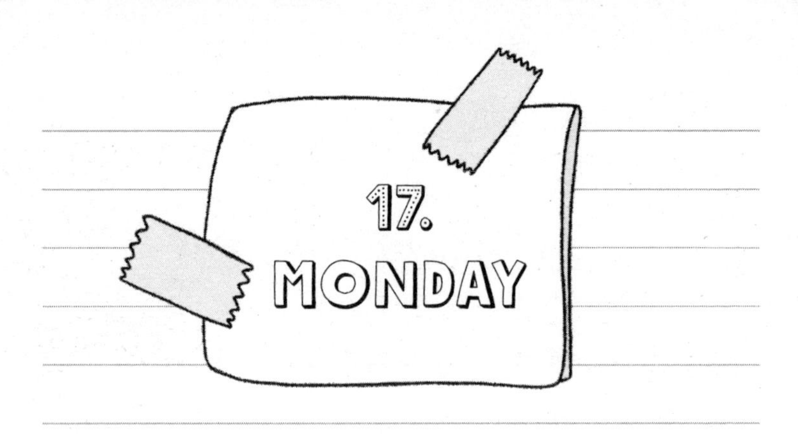

When I woke up I found a note stuck to my forehead.

Danny,

Guess what. I'VE GONE BACK TO FAIRYLAND TO GET RUFUS NOBEARD! Without his help you've got no chance of being a good Wizard of Doom. I'm not saying this to be mean, Danny. I'm just being honest. You've not even got a beard and you go red when teachers speak to you. Did you know you do that? Well, you do. Anyway, Rufus might not have a beard either, but he is a real wizard and he's better than nothing. If you really don't want him to help, then we can let him watch a bit of telly, give him some biscuits then send him back to Fairyland, OK?

See you soon . . . with a WIZARD!!!

From, S. Tink

P.S. I definitely think this is my next GOOD DEED. The moment you get on that stage and everyone sees you being a great wizard – BOOM! – the Mercorn 1000 will appear in my hand.

Now I've got to go to school knowing that Stink is in Fairyland hunting down her old pal, Rufus Nobeard. If you're wondering how Stink will fit a wizard through the fairy door, remember that she can shrink things down using her **YELLOW** spell.

I really, really hope she doesn't find Rufus Nobeard.

18.
SERIOUSLY BAD WIZARD NEWS

I am in massive trouble. I'm in such **MASSIVE** trouble that my hand is shaking – no – my **WHOLE BODY** is shaking – and it's **ALL** Stink's fault! I'm going to start at the beginning and tell you everything that's happened.

Stink might not have been at school with me, but it was still bad. I couldn't walk down the corridor without someone shouting, 'Oi, Disco Danny!'

As if that wasn't bad enough, I had Rufus Nobeard to worry about.

After school Kabir insisted on coming home with me to see if Stink had brought Rufus back from Fairyland. Apparently hanging out with a wizard is on Kabir's bucket list of things to do before he's old (thirty).

KABIR'S BUCKET LIST

- **Drink a can of Sprite in one go**

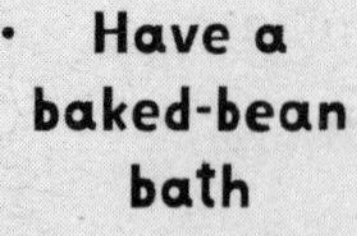

- **Have a baked-bean bath**

- **Get a pet giraffe**

I knew something was up when Dad asked me to check on Sophie because she was upstairs and had 'gone a bit quiet'.

When we burst into my bedroom, we saw this . . .

The wizard's eyes glowed like fire and his fingernails looked sharp enough to slice potatoes. He DEFINITELY had a beard. It was immense. In fact it was so big Sophie had made a den in it.

'Greetings, Daniel Todd,' said the wizard in a voice that sounded like thunder and rocks being mixed in a blender.

My name is Rufus Nobeard, and I am THE MOST FEARED WIZARD IN ALL OF FAIRYLAND!

At this point Stink emerged from where she had been hiding inside one of my trainers.

'I'm so sorry, Danny,' she said. 'Rufus has changed a bit since I last saw him.'

Leaving Kabir to look after Sophie, I took Stink into the bathroom for an urgent meeting. She told me that Rufus has not only grown since he was six but he has also become wicked. I asked why she'd brought him to meet me if she knew he was wicked and she said she had no choice because Rufus said he would put her in a sandwich and eat her if she didn't. Then she said that Rufus has committed unspeakable crimes against the fairy community and was wanted by the FBI.

'What's the FBI?' I said.

'The Fairy Bureau of Investigations,' she said. 'My brother, Fandango, works for them. He's their best agent. The FBI hunt the baddest of the bad baddies.'

I was so scared that my mouth went dry and I needed a wee.

Can't you shrink him down? I could stuff him in a sock then bundle him through the door.

Stink held up something that looked like a burnt match.

Look at my wand, Danny! I used up nearly all its magic shrinking Rufus to get him through the door. Unless I earn some nuggets and get my new wand, we're stuck with him!

Back in my bedroom, we discovered that Sophie had started plaiting Rufus Nobeard's beard and Kabir was wearing his pointy hat.

Rufus grinned wolfishly then said, 'Daniel Todd, I hear that you wish to be trained in the **DARK ARTS OF WIZARDRY***.'

'No. I don't,' I said.

'He definitely does,' said Kabir.

'Kabir, shut up,' I said, then I told the wizard that he had to go back to Fairyland right now. To show him I meant business I strode across the room, pointed at the fairy door and said, 'Go on. You've had your fun. Now off you go!'

*Rufus makes the end of his sentences go so loud that I can feel his voice vibrating in my toes.

The wizard looked at me for a moment then said, 'I don't think so, **DANIEL TODD**.'

Then he lay back on my bed and started reading one of my comics.

I'm writing this in the bathroom. Kabir has gone home – he didn't want to but Mum made him – and Sophie has gone to bed. It took ages because she had a tantrum when Dad wouldn't let 'Danny's wizard' read her bedtime stories. Right now Stink is having a bath, or rather a swim, to calm her down from the shock of nearly being eaten by her ex-best friend.

And me? I'm pretending to go to the toilet just so I can avoid going into my bedroom and seeing Rufus Nobeard.

Update . . .

HE'S GONE! Jas eventually forced me out of the bathroom and when I went into my bedroom it was empty.

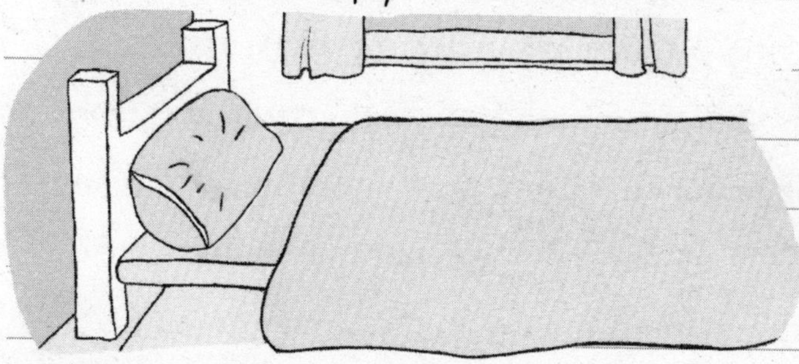

'He must have shrunk himself and gone back to Fairyland,' I said, remembering how forcefully I had told him to go.

'Yeah . . . maybe,' said Stink, but she didn't look convinced. Right now I don't care where Rufus Nobeard is as long as he isn't in my bedroom.

19. TUESDAY

Stink was suspiciously quiet at school today. During art she sat under my desk making a tiny pot out of a bit of clay, and in geography she watched a film about volcanoes from the safety of my hair. She was jumpy too. When Kabir slapped me on the back at the end of the day and shouted, '**WAAASSUUUUPPP**, Disco Danny?', she yelped like she was scared.

I guessed the experience with Rufus had freaked her out and I was pleased. Perhaps **NOW** she might stop bringing stuff out of Fairyland!

Also, everyone is **STILL** going on about my dance. My form group want Miss Nichols to put it in our assembly, but she said, 'The Wizard of Doom is definitely a non-dancing role.'

Anyway, Stink seemed to relax after school when we went to the tree house. Kabir, Stink and I drew comics, watched YouTube videos of hamsters falling off stuff when they're asleep (they're Stink's favourites) and then Stink used a new spell: **TANGERINE** to make Jasper Budgen's cat, Bailey, invisible.

Unfortunately her wand is so rubbish that the spell didn't work properly and you could still see its head.

I say unfortunately, but actually it was **FORTUNATE** because the floating cat head scared Jasper Budgen which is good because he's mean. Jasper is Professor Najin's other next-door neighbour (and Poppy and Fin's dad) and he once wrecked Najin's boat AND tried to get her foxes exterminated. That's why I didn't feel sorry for him when he saw Bailey's floating head, yelled, **'GHOST CAT!'**, then tripped over his sunbathing wife, Esther.

Next Stink used her **TANGERINE** spell to make a hole in my stomach then refused to do anything about it even after we heard Professor Najin's back door slam and footsteps approaching.

'Undo the spell, Stink!' I said. 'Najin's coming. She can't see me like this!'

'ENIREGNAT!' said Stink, and my stomach became solid seconds before a head appeared at the doorway of the tree house.

'HELLO, CHILDREN!' said a booming voice. 'WOULD YOU CARE FOR SOME BISCUITS?'

It wasn't Professor Najin . . . IT WAS RUFUS NOBEARD!!!!!!!

Questions flooded my mind, like . . .

Why was he in Professor Najin's house?
Why was he wearing one of her aprons . . . and a tracksuit?
Why was ajin's whistle nging around his neck?
Where had his beard gone?
Why was e holding a plate of biscuits?

And – my biggest question of all – **WHERE WAS PROFESSOR NAJIN?**

'What have you done with Professor Najin?' I cried.

Rufus Nobeard grinned and wriggled his eyebrows wickedly. For one terrible moment I wondered if he had melted her, or frozen her, or worse, but then Professor Najin wandered out on to the patio. 'Hello, boys!' she shouted. 'I see you've met my new lodger.' Then she started cutting her hair with a pair of nail scissors.

Was it true? Was Rufus Nobeard, the most feared wizard in all of Fairyland, Professor Najin's new lodger? It didn't make sense. Professor Najin is a sensible lady who loves living on her own. How did Rufus Nobeard persuade her to let him move in?

It's important that you know that I didn't say that last sentence out loud, I THOUGHT it in my head, but even so, Rufus Nobeard replied . . .

All I needed to do was steal her most precious item – this whistle. I acquired a sporty look, bumped into her then casually asked to see her whistle. The moment it was in my hands Professor Najin fell **UNDER MY SPELL!**

Wait, how did you know what I was thinking?

Rufus did a smug smile. 'I read your mind. I can also temporarily mesmerise people by wriggling my fingers which is how I was able to acquire this tracksuit from an emporium named Sports Direct and how I got my beard trimmed for free at Gayle's Nails. They are just two of my **INCREDIBLY POWERFUL SKILLS!**'

'Mate,' said Kabir. 'Please can you stop shouting? You're scaring the fairy.'

It was true. Stink was trembling on Kabir's shoulder.

Rufus Nobeard grinned. 'I love scaring fairies,' he said, then he reached for his wand.

Quick as a flash, Stink flew close to his face and snarled, 'If you're mean to me, Rufus Nobeard, then I will tell Danny and Kabir what you did in Year Two when your mum forgot to put a note in your lunchbox!'

20. BAD BOY BISCUITS

For a few minutes things were tense in the tree house. Stink glared at Rufus and Rufus's fingers twitched over his wand. In the end Kabir broke the ice by asking Rufus if he could have a biscuit.

'Have one . . . **IF YOU DARE!**' cackled Rufus. 'Some of my bakes are so deadly that one crumb could turn you into a slug **FOR ETERNITY!**'

Kabir hesitated . . .

Are these biscuits one of your deadly bakes?

'No,' admitted Rufus.

'They're nice!' said Kabir as he chomped on one. 'Am I getting coconut?'

'And chocolate,' said Rufus with a snarl.

'How come you're baking, Rufus?' asked Stink. Since she had stood up to him she seemed less afraid of him.

Rufus narrowed his eyes then said, 'Although Najin is totally under my spell she would only agree to my request for lodging if I agreed to do all the cooking. This is not a problem because being an excellent chef is another of my **INCREDIBLY POWERFUL SKILLS!'**

He wasn't joking, the biscuits were great.

Stink fluttered around the tree house and said, 'Seeing as you're sticking around, you can teach Danny to be a good wizard.'

Rufus didn't have to help me, but I could see he was tempted. I guess it was another opportunity for him to show off his **INCREDIBLY POWERFUL SKILLS.**

He fixed his blazing eyes on me and said, 'How about it, Daniel Todd? Are you ready to be trained in the dark arts of wizardry?'

I wasn't, but I was sick of people dancing in my face as I walked down the corridor at school. I imagined glaring at everyone in Year 7, just like Rufus was glaring at me now. With his help, I really could be amazing in the school assembly.

'I'm ready,' I said, putting out my hand. 'But you've got to promise that you won't make me look stupid. Everyone at school thinks I'm a massive loser.' I paused here to glare at Stink. 'So only teach me cool, awesome stuff.'

Rufus grinned showing sharp teeth and said, 'ALL my stuff is cool and awesome . . . **AND BAD!**'

His last words made Kabir, Stink and I shoot nervous glances at each other, but I still reached forward to shake Rufus's gigantic hand.

'Tomorrow, Daniel Todd, your training shall begin!' he cried. 'Perhaps I will teach you to do magic **LIKE THIS!**'

Then he whipped out his wand, bellowed, '**GELATA MAGICAE!**' and encased Stink in jelly.

She's only just finished eating her way out.

21. WIZARD EYES

We had our first rehearsal during form time today and I was a rubbish wizard. I couldn't remember my words and I tripped over my pointy shoes (which Miss Nichol says are perfect for my wizard costume). Finally, when I pointed my staff at Nelly the Element (Mara) and shouted, '**BEGONE!**', Poppy Budgen shouted out, 'Calm down, Disco Danny!' and everyone laughed.

Because of this, I was looking forward to my lesson with Rufus Nobeard.

We met in Professor Najin's garden. I was nervous. It didn't help that Kabir, Stink and Sophie had decided to watch from the tree house.

To begin with Rufus strutted around giving me a lecture.

A wizard starts from within, Danny. You must feel the power. What do you feel right here?
The Frosties that I had when I got in from school?

'NO!' he bellowed at the top of his voice. 'You feel the fire of a thousand dragons burning in your core. Now unleash that deadly power!'

Honestly, I didn't have a clue what he was on about. 'What?' I said.

Rufus hissed, 'Copy me.'

For the next hour he showed me how to . . .

1. STAND LIKE A WIZARD

Stand with your chest sticking out and one leg slightly in front of the other. Grasp staff or wand and place other hand on hip.

2. STARE LIKE A WIZARD

Raise chin, flare nostrils (like you are sniffing something big and evil) then DON'T BLINK. If you do have to show weakness and blink, do it so fast no one notices.

3. BELLOW LIKE A WIZARD

- Speak from the bottom of your stomach. Go as low as you dare. If in doubt, speak from your bottom, but make sure the sound travels upwards.
- If you can't think of anything wicked to say, stroke your beard and narrow your eyes.
- If you STILL can't think of anything wicked to say, bellow . . .

SILENCE!

I think it went well. Afterwards I asked the others what they thought. Kabir said I was definitely louder than before and Sophie said I was 'a bit scary'.

22. THURSDAY

PIG BUBBLE!

DIG RUBBLE!

STIG NUBBLE!

In our 7N assembly rehearsal today, I couldn't say the line:

I AM THE WIZARD OF DOOM AND YOU, NELLY THE ELEMENT, ARE IN BIG TROUBLE!

Fin Budgen said I was rubbish and tried to get all of 7N to sit down and go on strike until Miss Nichol sacked me as the Wizard of Doom and gave him the part instead.

It didn't work.

Things got worse in assembly. Mrs Busby showed us a new video she had made. It was called, Making the Right Decisions at MOS Academy. To start off with there was happy guitar music playing over a series of clips of students doing good stuff like:

Playing the flute

Opening doors

Picking up litter

Handing in homework

I noticed that Fin and Poppy Budgen featured in three of the videos.

Then the music changed and became sad and there were clips of students making bad decisions. Mainly these had come from grainy CCTV footage.

Dropping litter

White socks . . . NO!

But the last film was crystal clear. It showed me wriggling around on the stage as the foxes tickled me.

Somehow Mrs Busby had slowed the film down and the caption underneath said . . .

Showing off to your friends

It's fair to say all of Year 7 enjoyed Mrs Busby's film. Kabir laughed so hard some Weetabix came out of his nose. 'Sorry, mate,' he said. 'It's just so funny!'

That was the moment when I knew that I HAD to make the wizard plan work. If my best friend thought I was a joke then it was time to take urgent action!

The minute the bell rang at the end of the day, I sprinted out of school.

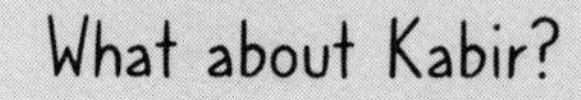

What about Kabir?
We can't wait for him. This is an emergency!

I ran all the way to Professor Najin's where I found Rufus Nobeard snapping the heads off flowers.

'Teach me everything you know,' I said. 'Even my best friend is laughing at me!'

'I'm not surprised with that pipsqueak voice,' said Rufus. 'Today we will work on improving your bellow.'

He sat in a deckchair holding a drink with ice cubes and got me to bellow, 'I am the Wizard of Doom and you, Nelly the Element, are in big trouble!' again and again until I made the ice cubes in his glass tremble.

I am the Wizard of Doom and you, Nelly the Element, are in big trouble!

When I finally managed to do it, Rufus grinned showing his white teeth and said, 'Excellent!'

Then he added, 'I am tempted to take you back to Fairyland to train you as my apprentice. All the best wizards have an apprentice*, a sidekick to laugh at their jokes and help them mix up deadly potions. You could be my very own funny little fellow!'

'No way!' I said.

*Stink says this is true and has given me this list of famous wizards and their apprentices . . .

Johnny Erasmus and Pickles (cat apprentice)

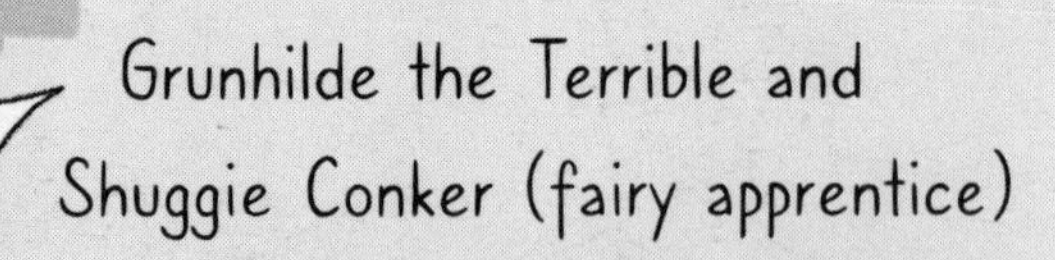

Grunhilde the Terrible and Shuggie Conker (fairy apprentice)

Margery L'awful and Ambrose L'awful (giant husband apprentice)

23.
MR NOBEARD

BIG NEWS!

Kabir and I walked into our form room this morning and found Miss Nichol talking to . . .

RUFUS NOBEARD!!!

Up in my hair Stink yelped, and I was so shocked I blurted out, 'What are **YOU** doing here?'

'Danny!' said Miss Nichol. 'That's no way to talk to a new member of staff.'

A NEW MEMBER OF STAFF? What was Miss Nichol on about? Then I noticed Rufus was wearing a lab coat over his tracksuit and arranging science equipment on a trolley.

Miss Nichol explained that Mr Nobeard was her new lab technician.

'Young Daniel is my neighbour,' explained Rufus Nobeard. 'He knows how much I enjoy making potions.' Then he winked at me and mouthed, 'Poisonous ones.'

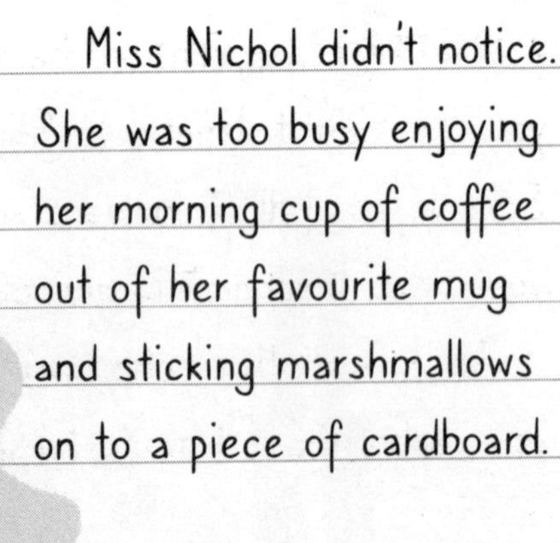

Miss Nichol didn't notice. She was too busy enjoying her morning cup of coffee out of her favourite mug and sticking marshmallows on to a piece of cardboard.

'Look, Danny,' she said. 'I've nearly finished your beard. Just one week to go until the assembly.'

'Great . . .' I said as I stared at the beard. I knew I would look ridiculous wearing a marshmallow beard, but right now I had bigger things to worry about, like Miss Nichol's new lab assistant, Mr Nobeard.

I left Miss Nichol dipping marshmallows in her coffee and cornered Rufus Nobeard by the cupboard.

'Seriously,' I said. 'What are you doing here?'

'I've decided to be the first wizard to have a **HUMAN** apprentice,' he said. 'And if you won't do it, I need to find another one. Schools are full of humans so I mesmerised your head teacher into giving me this job.'

'No one at this school will be your apprentice,' I said sternly.

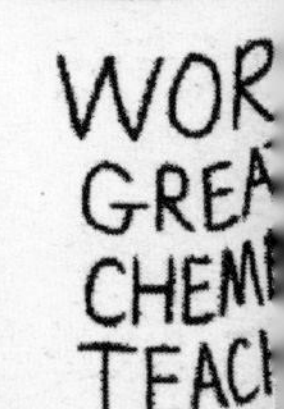

But Rufus Nobeard just grinned and said, 'We'll see!'

I joined Kabir and Stink.

This is terrible. MOS Academy have employed an evil wizard and it's all my fault!

And mine!

But, looking on the bright side, MOS Academy have employed an evil wizard . . . How cool is that? And he's our mate!

It's not cool, Kabir. He told me that he's going to try and find an apprentice, and look – he's in the cupboard licking Miss Nichol's Maltesers and putting them back in the bag. He can't stop being bad!

Whenever I caught sight of Rufus during the rest of the day, he was up to something . . . something wicked . . .

24. MISS NICHOL, THE WIZARD'S APPRENTICE

After school, Kabir asked if I wanted to come to the park to meet up with Cooper, Mara and Lamb Dog. I was tempted, but I knew I needed to go home and practise my lines.

'But I want to see Lamb Dog!' moaned Stink as we headed up the road. I did too, but our assembly was next week and I needed to work on speaking and glaring at the same time.

I was halfway up the road when a voice boomed out . . .

DANIEL TODD!
WAIT FOR ME!

'Oh no,' said Stink. 'It's Rufus. What does he want?'

'I don't know,' I said. 'We haven't got wizard training tonight.'

Rufus looked particularly magical striding towards us, so I decided to make a run for it. But I'd only taken a few steps when Rufus glued me to the spot by yelling, '**LENTUM PUERI!**'

It was like my shoe was cemented to the pavement. Rufus only undid the spell when he caught up with us.

'Leave Danny alone, Rufus,' said Stink. 'Everyone at school already thinks he's stupid because of his dance and now you're making him walk home with a teacher.'

'**SILENCE!**' he said, then he told me this . . .

'I have decided to make Miss Nichol my wizard apprentice, Danny. The way she eats her hummus and cucumber sandwiches delights me! Have you noticed how she gives students work then goes into her cupboard to drink Fanta? So cunning! Her eyes are the colour of poison. Her lips are the colour of elves, and by that I mean the most delicate shade of coral. She can silence the cheekiest of students with a glare and a sarcastic comment – what a sorceress! **AND** she is a master of potions.'

'She's a chemistry teacher!' I said, but Rufus wasn't interested in the truth.

'**SILENCE!**' he said, then he grabbed my shoulder and looked into my eyes.

I know that Fairyland will fall under her spell, just as I have. I can see the future so clearly, Danny. Miss Nichol will come to Fairyland with me and become my apprentice. When she is trained, we will rule Fairyland together. With her brutal stare and knowledge of chemistry and my beard and magical skills we will be unstoppable!

Up in my hair, Stink made her feelings clear. 'This is **TERRIBLE**, Danny! Everyone in Fairyland WILL love Miss Nichol because her lips ARE the colour of elves. We can't let her become his apprentice!'

I agreed with Stink, but I wasn't too worried.

'There's no way Miss Nichol will agree to becoming your apprentice,' I told Rufus. 'She loves being our form teacher. Plus she's got a boyfriend called Scott. He's a computer programmer and he loves *Star Wars* and Live Action Role Play, just like her. She'd never leave Scott to go to Fairyland with you!'

'Scott!' Rufus spat. 'Whoever this Scott is, I WILL DESTROY HIM!'

Then he marched towards Professor Najin's house.

Up in my hair, Stink said, 'Uh-oh . . . poor Scott.'

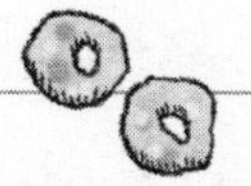
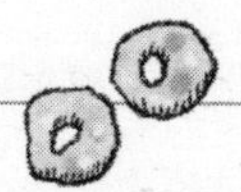

25. SCOTT-WATCHING

Rufus Nobeard has disappeared. Professor Najin says that he's gone birdwatching, but I don't believe that for one minute.

'I bet he's gone Scott-watching,' I said to Stink. 'Come with me and help me find him.'

No way! I'm going to Dinotropolis soft play with Sophie. She's smuggling me there in her backpack.

So I messaged Kabir to ask him if he wanted to look for Rufus Nobeard. He replied with this message:

But I couldn't go to the skatepark, not when I knew Rufus might be out there, terrorising Scott. Plus, I could see some scary skater kids in the picture and I knew some of them would have watched the Disco Danny film.

Stink decided what I should do.

Come to DINOTROPOLIS SOFT PLAY with me and Sophie then we can look for Scott afterwards.

I can't relax if I think Rufus is out there doing something bad to Scott. You need to tell me **ALL** the crimes Rufus Nobeard had committed in Fairyland so I know just how wicked he is.

And that's when Stink showed me this FBI wanted poster.

WANTED

EVIL WIZARD AND ALL-ROUND BAD EGG

NOBEARD'S CRIMES INCLUDE:

- SHOE THEFT
- PUSHING A TROLL INTO A SWAMP
- TRICKING A UNICORN INTO DETANGLING HIS BEARD
- REMOVING MERMAIDS FROM THEIR CASTLE
- MOVING INTO THE MERMAIDS' CASTLE
- ADDING AN EXTENSION TO THE MERMAIDS' CASTLE WITHOUT PROPER PLANNING PERMISSION

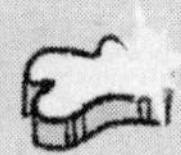

I said that his crimes didn't sound that bad, but then Stink told me exactly how he'd removed the mermaids from their castle and just how many shoes he had stolen.

Still, Rufus had never exploded anyone or made them disappear, so I went off to Dinotropolis feeling a bit less worried about Scott.

Stink **LOVED** Dinotropolis because I got stuck in a slide and Sophie took her clothes off in the ball pit then ran away from Mum.

I did lose Stink for half an hour, but I found her trapped inside a T-rex.

On the way home we were driving past the park on the outskirts of town when I spotted an elf eating a KFC.

'Stop the car!' I yelled to Mum. 'I want to walk home.'

But Stink wasn't happy. 'Danny,' she snapped, as I walked us into the shady woods. 'What are we doing in these rubbish trees? I'm tired. I want to watch telly with Soph!'

'We're checking up on Scott,' I said.

26.
SCOTT THE VIKING-NINJA-DEMON

I followed the KFC elf to a clearing then hid behind a tree.

'WHAT is going on, Danny?' said Stink.

It's hard to describe what we could see so I have drawn a picture to give you the general idea. Basically, a load of grown-ups were dressed up and having a fight. It was awesome.

Soon I spotted Miss Nichol. She was sitting on a deckchair, reading a magazine and drinking bubble tea.

'There's Rufus!' squeaked Stink. She was right. Rufus Nobeard was lurking in the bushes behind Miss Nichol.

We inched our way through the trees until we were standing next to him. He didn't notice us. He was too busy staring at the fighting grown-ups.

'What are you doing, Rufus!' I hissed.

He jumped and cried, 'Mermaids' scales*!', but he recovered quickly.

Look at Miss Nichol, Danny! She is obviously the queen of this motley crew. See how she sits on her throne drinking some sort of wicked brew from a goblet! She is overseeing the battle, possibly controlling it with her mind, or by using the book of spells that she is perusing.

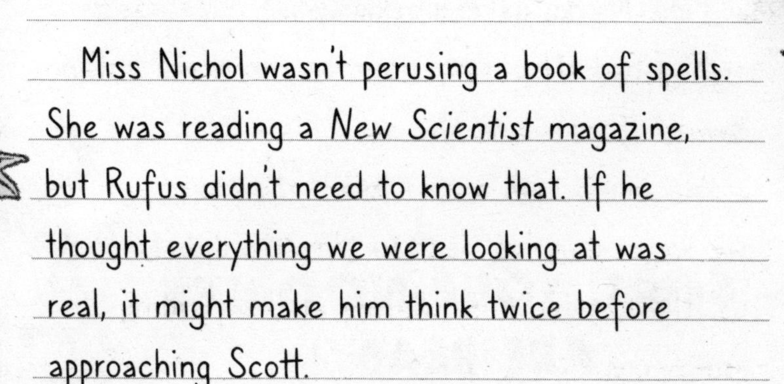

Miss Nichol wasn't perusing a book of spells. She was reading a *New Scientist* magazine, but Rufus didn't need to know that. If he thought everything we were looking at was real, it might make him think twice before approaching Scott.

But where was Scott?

*Mermaids' scales is a mega-rude swear word in Fairyland. If you meet a magical person, **DON'T** say it.

Miss Nichol gave him away.

She had a camping stove on the grass. Putting down her magazine she gave the contents of a pan a prod with a twig then bellowed . . .

Scott! YOUR NOODLES ARE READY!

'Aha!' cackled Rufus. 'Get ready to meet your nemesis, Scott!' Then he pointed his wand into the clearing.

At that moment, one of the LARPers set off a smoke bomb and from a billowing cloud of green smoke stepped . . . Scott.

Scott looked terrifying. Plus, as he strode towards Miss Nichol he took out a goblin, a wolf girl and some sort of root elf. They fell

to the ground and pretended to die loudly and dramatically.

Rufus slipped his wand back into his pocket.

'Aren't you going to fight him?' said Stink.

Rufus took a step back. 'Not today.'

'Does that mean you've given up on the idea of making Miss Nichol your apprentice?' I asked.

Rufus glared at me. 'Have you lost your mind, Daniel Todd? Of course I haven't! Look at her. She is **MAGNIFICENT**. Scott is trembling at her feet, yet she doesn't even glance at him!'

Scott was trembling because he was trying to eat noodles while trapped in a complicated costume and Miss Nichol wasn't looking at him because she was clearly gripped by her magazine.

Rufus said, 'Miss Nichol is **EXACTLY** the sort of human being I, Rufus Nobeard, deserve as my apprentice!'

Then he went, 'Mwahahaha!' But quieter than usual, before walking back home with us.

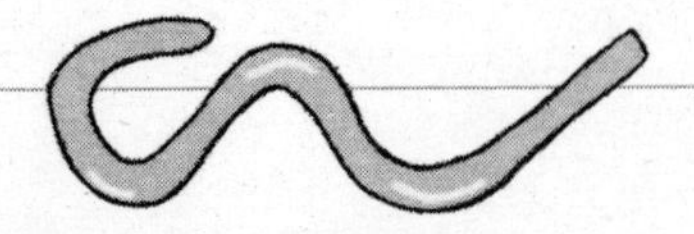

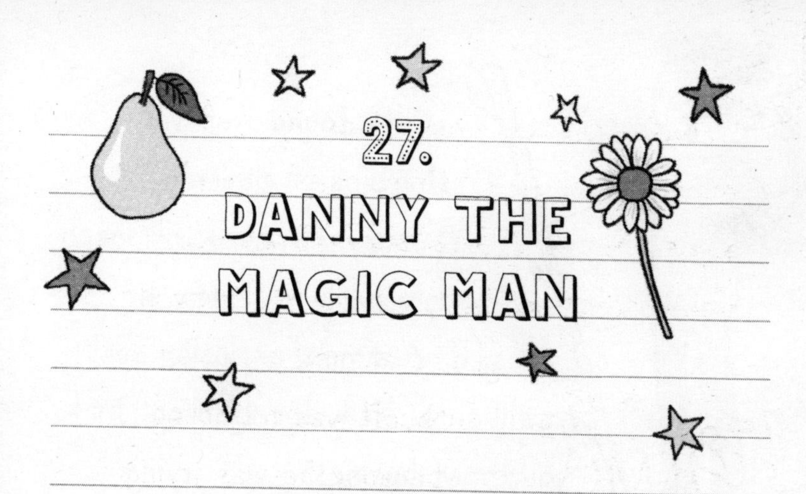

27. DANNY THE MAGIC MAN

Kabir turned up after breakfast this morning wanting to show me a rap that he's written to perform in our assembly.

'Sorry,' I said, 'but I'm supposed to be round at Najin's. Rufus is going to show me how to do **REAL** magic.'

'My rap is even better than magic,' he grumbled as he followed me out of the house.

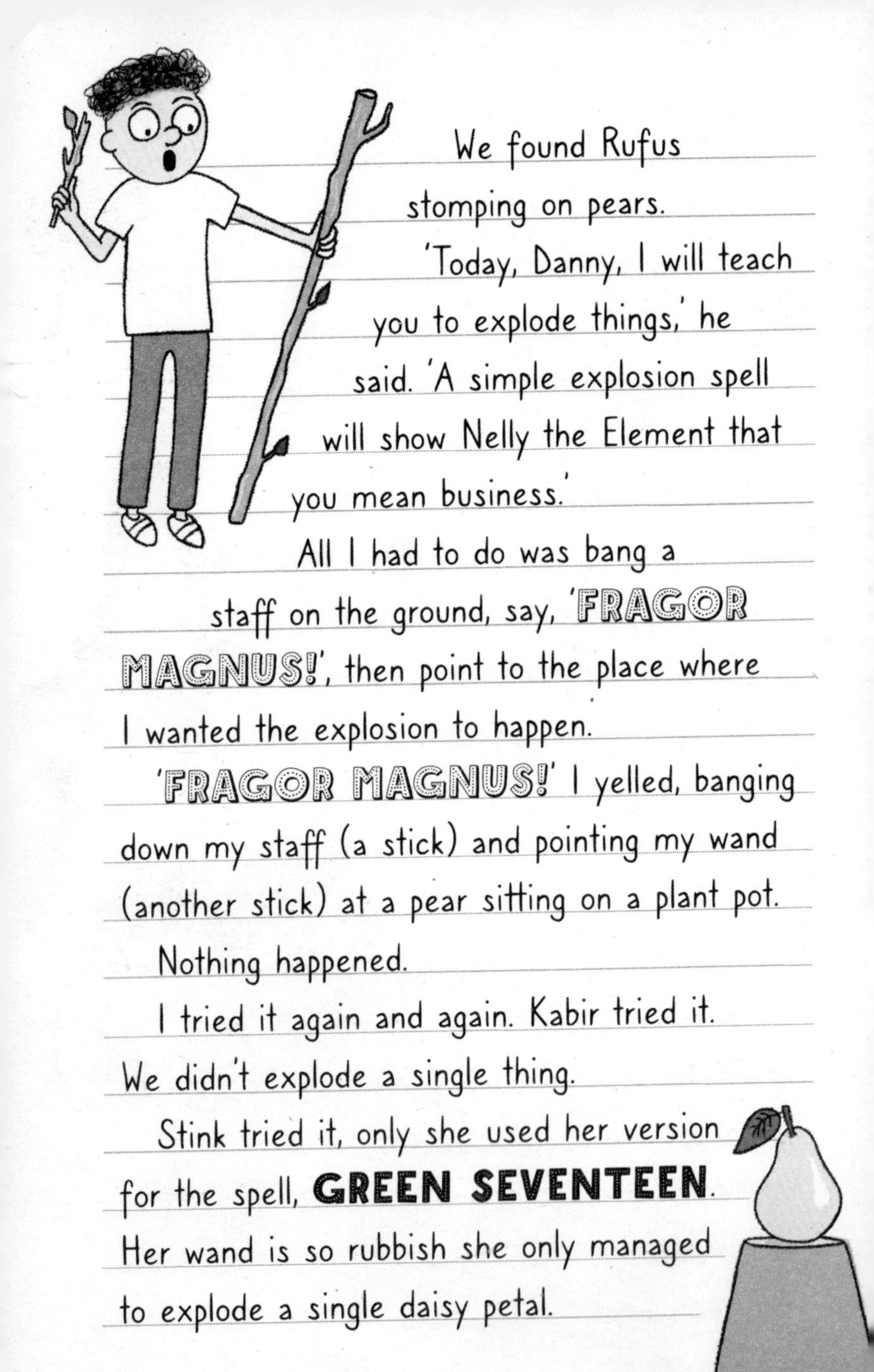

We found Rufus stomping on pears.

'Today, Danny, I will teach you to explode things,' he said. 'A simple explosion spell will show Nelly the Element that you mean business.'

All I had to do was bang a staff on the ground, say, '**FRAGOR MAGNUS!**', then point to the place where I wanted the explosion to happen.

'**FRAGOR MAGNUS!**' I yelled, banging down my staff (a stick) and pointing my wand (another stick) at a pear sitting on a plant pot.

Nothing happened.

I tried it again and again. Kabir tried it. We didn't explode a single thing.

Stink tried it, only she used her version for the spell, **GREEN SEVENTEEN**. Her wand is so rubbish she only managed to explode a single daisy petal.

In the end Rufus said we were 'worse than unicorns' at magic and stomped back into Professor Najin's house.

I flopped down on the grass.

'If I can't do magic, I'm going to be a hopeless wizard,' I said.

'Don't worry, mate,' said Kabir. 'Remember it's just an assembly.'

That was easy for Kabir to say. He wasn't being called Disco Danny every day.

Kabir wanted to go out on the SUP board, but I didn't feel like it. I was too worried about the assembly so instead I went home and spent the afternoon trying to make a Lego man explode.

I didn't manage it, but I did make him a cool car which Stink is currently driving around my bedroom.

Goodnight, diary. I'm sad that I didn't do any magic today, but I'm not giving up yet!

28.
FANDANGO

So much **DRAMA** happened today.

It all kicked off at six thirty this morning when my bedroom was raided by the FBI.

That's right. **MY BEDROOM WAS RAIDED BY THE FBI.**

I was woken by a bright light being shone in my eyes. The light was beaming out of a wand, but the fairy holding the wand wasn't Stink . . .

. . . it was Stink's brother!

'Fandango?' I said.

'It's Special Agent F.Tink to you!' he snarled as he landed on my forehead.

Suddenly Fandango yelled, '**RIGIDUM CORPUS!**' and I went as stiff as a plank of wood. Luckily I could still move my mouth so we were able to have this conversation . . .

What do you want? Why are you in my bedroom?

I ask the questions, boy. I believe you have been hiding the wanted wizard criminal, Rufus Nobeard. Where is he?!

Just then tiny voice hissed in my ear . . .

Don't tell him **ANYTHING**, Danny! I'll get in so much trouble if the FBI find out I brought Rufus here!

So I said . . .

Rufus who-beard? I don't know what you're talking about.

Oh, really?

Yes, really!

Then why did a gnome report seeing a wizard and a 'yellow-haired fairy' going through **YOUR** fairy door?

Maybe the gnome made it up?

If that's true, then why is this hairbrush full of WIZARD BEARD-HAIR?

Flipping Sophie and her wizard grooming! For a moment, I didn't know what to say, but Stink came to my rescue.

She shot out of my hair and cried, 'Because I took the hairbrush back to Fairyland and brushed a wizard's beard with it. Let my boy go, Fandango. He's done nothing wrong!'

'*Let my boy go!*' Fandango said, mimicking Stink. Then he pointed his wand at Stink and said, 'I should have known **YOU'D** be involved in this. **FRAGOR MAGNUS!**'

A ball of fire shot out of Fandango's wand, hitting Stink in the stomach.

She flew back, bounced off the wall then landed on my bed.

'Keep your mouth shut, rubbish-wings,' said Fandango. 'You never have anything good to say!'

Now this made me angry. My sister Sophie has done some bad stuff to me. She's drawn cats on my bedroom wall, put Peppa Pig toys in my school bag and she regularly dresses up our dog, Frida, in my pants, but I would NEVER do an exploding spell on Soph or call her names. She's my little sister and that means I have to look after her no matter how annoying she is.

'Hey!' I mumbled through my frozen lips. 'Don't talk to Stink like –'

Before I could say another word, Fandango yelled, '**FRAGOR MAGNUS!**', and a ball of fire hit me on the nose.

'I'll speak to my big-haired, no-magic, mouldy-toed sister however I like,' said Fandango. 'And if I find out that you've been lying to me about Rufus Nobeard you are in **BIG TROUBLE**, boy!'

Then he flew out of the open window.

Luckily Fandango's 'rigidum corpus' spell wore off in time for me to get ready for school.

'Thanks for not telling Fandango about Rufus,' said Stink as we hurried to meet Kabir.

'That's OK,' I said, forcing my still-stiff limbs to move as fast as possible. 'Do you think Fandango will find him?'

Part of me was hoping he would. It would be a weight off my mind if Rufus was taken back to Fairyland.

'I doubt it,' said Stink. 'Humanyworld is massive and Fandango is tiny.'

The last thing Stink said before we met up with Kabir was . . .

I haven't really got mouldy toes, Danny.
I know.

29. THE WIZARD'S APPRENTICE

We didn't have time to rehearse on Monday because we had an extra assembly on uniform. After the assembly, Miss Nichol reminded us that we were performing Nelly the Element and the Wizard of Doom on **FRIDAY** (like I could forget) and that we've only got three more form times to rehearse.

But I don't know my words, or what to do, or anything!
Don't worry. I know that you're going to be really funny, Danny. Everyone will love you!

I'm starting to wonder if Miss Nichol has forgotten why she made me the Wizard of Doom in the first place. I don't want people to think I'm **REALLY FUNNY**. They already think that! I want them to think I'm **COOL** and **IMPRESSIVE**.

Stink cheered me up by telling me that if I forget my lines, she can whisper them to me from my hair.

At lunchtime Stink told Rufus that Fandango was looking for him. He didn't seem bothered. All he said was, 'I eat fairies like him for breakfast!'.

But the biggest news happened AFTER school.

Kabir and I were walking home when Rufus Nobeard caught up with us.

'Ah, children and fairy,' he said, stroking his beard wickedly. 'A word, if I may.'

We didn't have much choice. We knew that if we tried to get away he'd freeze us to the spot or encase us in jelly.

'What do you want, Rufus?' Stink piped up from my hair.

'I want to ask a question about my future apprentice,' he said.

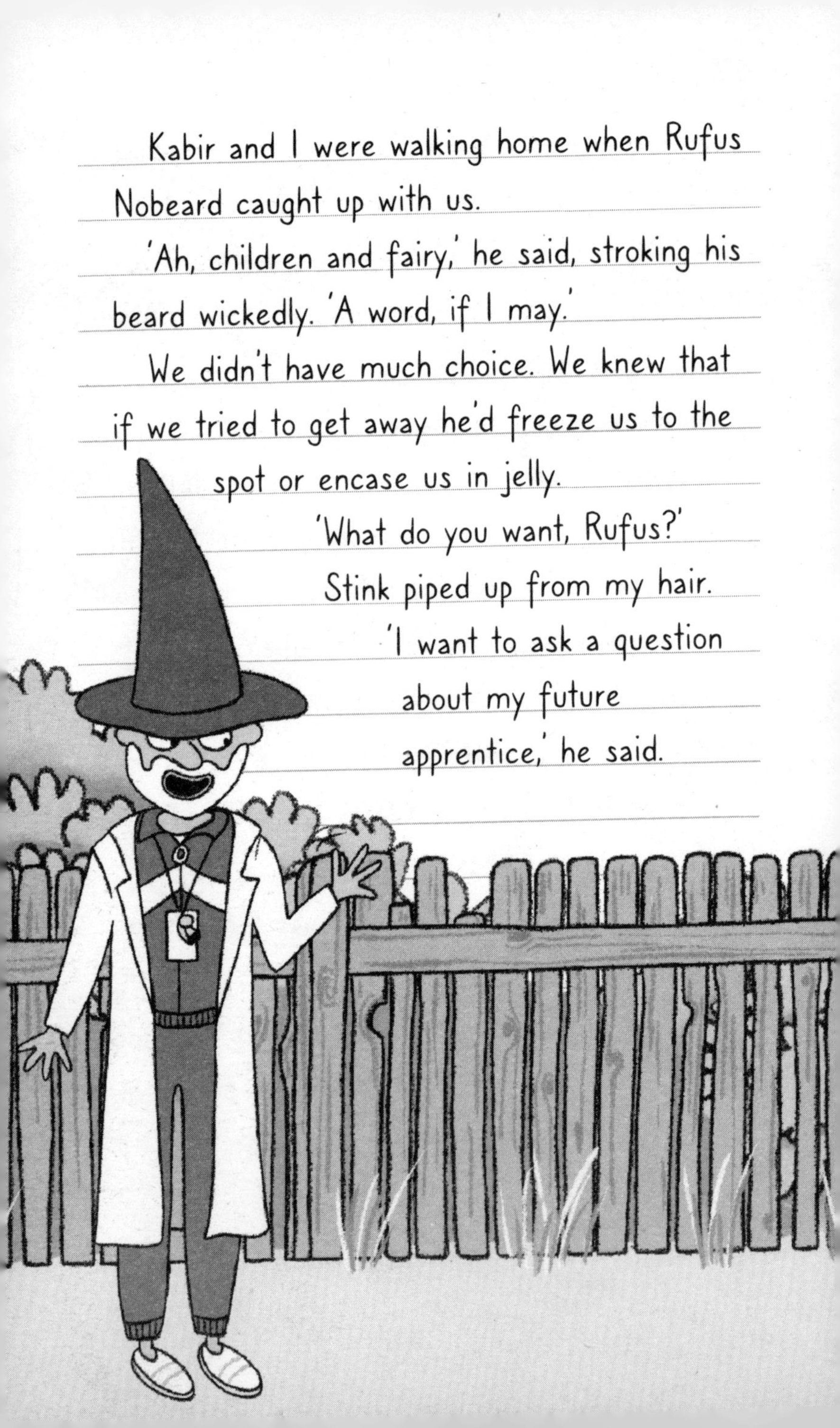

'Listen, Rufus,' I said – no way was I calling him Mr Nobeard out of school – 'Miss Nichol will NEVER go to Fairyland with you. She loves being our form teacher and doing Live Action Role Play with Scott.'

'Innnn-ter-es-ting,' he said, like that, all drawn out. Then he touched Professor Najin's whistle and added, 'Out of curiosity, what else does Miss Nichol love?'

Straight away I knew what he was up to. He was planning to steal something precious to Miss Nichol so he could put her under his spell!

Unfortunately Stink and Kabir didn't catch on as quickly as me.

Maltesers?

Chemistry?

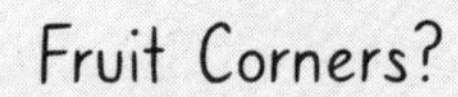

Fruit Corners?

Bunsen burners?

Ed Sheeran?

Then Kabir said something terrible . . .

I know what she loves most in the world –

Don't say it, Kabir!

Her World's Greatest Chemistry Teacher mug!

'Oh yeah!' said Stink. 'She loves that mug. I heard her say she takes it with her on holiday.'

'And when Mr Gibson borrowed it without asking she locked him in his classroom for twenty minutes,' added Kabir.

'Innnn-ter-es-ting . . .' said Rufus, but even slower this time. Then he grinned, showing sharp teeth, and darted into Professor Najin's house.

Once he was gone I said, 'Why did you say that? If Rufus gets hold of Miss Nichol's mug she'll be under his spell and he'll have no problem persuading her to become his apprentice!'

'Whoops,' said Stink.

Kabir looked worried too, but he reckons Miss Nichol is safe because she **NEVER** lets the mug out of her sight.

I just hope he's right . . .

30. MR NOBEARD THE LEGEND

We only had **FIVE MINUTES** to rehearse today. I had another go at doing the **FRAGOR MAGNUS** explosion spell, but the only thing that happened was an awkward silence and Miss Nichol saying, 'Stick to the script, Danny.'

After the rehearsal, Miss Nichol showed us the costumes we were going to wear. Just like she promised, she'd made them all herself, but they don't look anything like her Zandra costume . . .

Nelly the Element is going to wear this

Her gang (including Kabir) are wearing this

And I'm wearing this

It's terrible! My cloak is **Scott'S OLD DRESSING GOWN** and my staff is a stale baguette wrapped in silver foil. I look more like a lazy baker than a wizard.

If I go on stage dressed like that I'll be eaten alive!

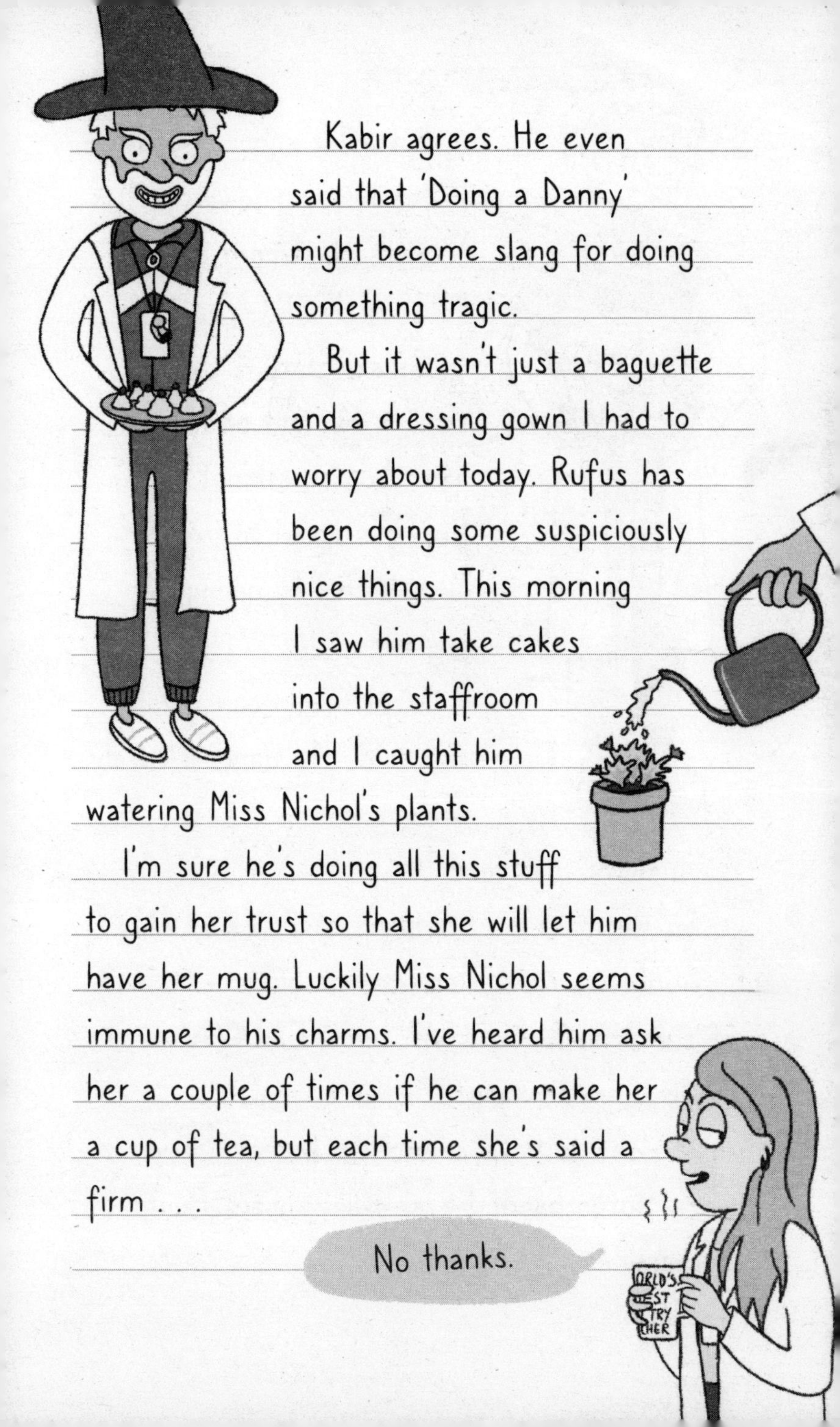

Kabir agrees. He even said that 'Doing a Danny' might become slang for doing something tragic.

But it wasn't just a baguette and a dressing gown I had to worry about today. Rufus has been doing some suspiciously nice things. This morning I saw him take cakes into the staffroom and I caught him watering Miss Nichol's plants.

I'm sure he's doing all this stuff to gain her trust so that she will let him have her mug. Luckily Miss Nichol seems immune to his charms. I've heard him ask her a couple of times if he can make her a cup of tea, but each time she's said a firm . . .

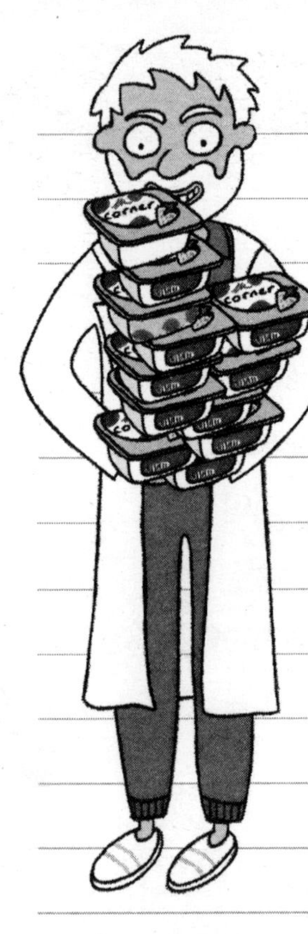

But after school I spotted Rufus heading towards Miss Nichol's classroom carrying TWELVE Fruit Corners.

'Quick, Stink,' I said, shaking her out of my hair. 'Do something! Rufus is about to impress Miss Nichol by giving her yoghurt.'

'What magic can I do?' she said. 'My wand is barely working.'

'Just try,' I begged.

So she cast her shrinking spell: **YELLOW!**

Stink was right. Her wand is busted. Instead of shrinking Rufus's gift, her **YELLOW** spell made it grow!

You should have seen Miss Nichol's face when Rufus handed over twelve giant Fruit Corners.

'Thank you, Mr Nobeard,' she said. 'I LOVE Fruit Corners. Where did you get them from?'

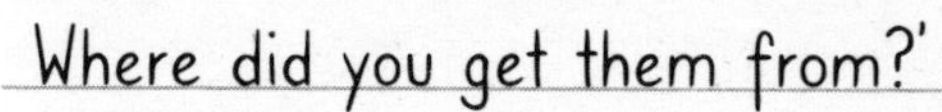

'A little place I know called Fairyland,' he said. 'I think you would like it there.'

Then Miss Nichol said . . .

But Rufus wasn't listening. He was eyeing Miss Nichol's mug which was sitting on top of her pile of marking.

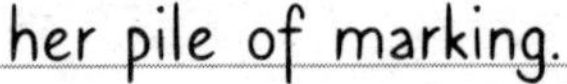

All this happened earlier and now we're at home. I can't let Rufus Nobead get his pointy-nailed hands on Miss Nichol's mug! I've just asked Stink if there is any way she can shrink Rufus down so we can send him back to Fairyland, but she says it's too risky.

Think about it, Danny. My wand is totally unreliable. If I made the yoghurts grow, I might make Rufus grow. Then he'd be extra powerful! Just make sure you're an amazing wizard on Friday and then I'll get my Mercorn 1000. The second that wand is in my hand I **PROMISE** I will get rid of Rufus.

How can you be so sure that me being an amazing wizard is your good deed?

We're not supposed to tell our humans this, Danny, but if fairies working for F.A.R.T. get stuck then Melville sends us a clue. I found **THIS** inside the fairy door the other day.

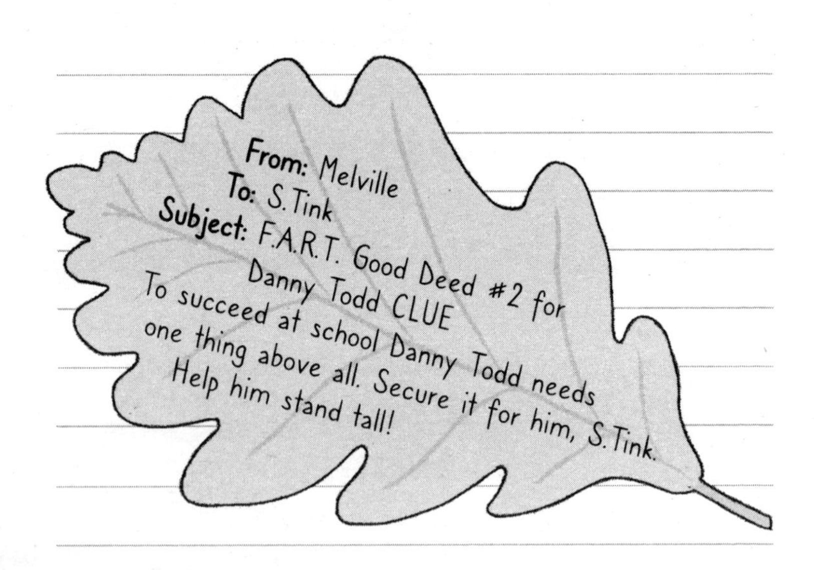

From: Melville
To: S.Tink
Subject: F.A.R.T. Good Deed #2 for
Danny Todd CLUE
To succeed at school Danny Todd needs
one thing above all. Secure it for him, S.Tink.
Help him stand tall!

'It's obvious,' said Stink. 'I have to help you be a good wizard!'

I think she's right. If I do well on Friday then everything will change: I can stop feeling embarrassed, Stink will earn her nuggets and we can stop Nobeard from making Miss Nichol his apprentice.

It's all down to me. I **HAVE** to learn my lines!!!

31.
BAD HAT

I wasn't an amazing wizard during rehearsals today. Instead I got stuck in my hat and Miss Nichol had to cut me out. She's given me an alternative wizard's hat that she says looks 'super magical', but I'm not convinced.

Meanwhile, Rufus continued to try to impress Miss Nichol **AND** get his hands on her mug.

Today he gave her a swanky pencil sharpener and the latest edition of *New Scientist* magazine.

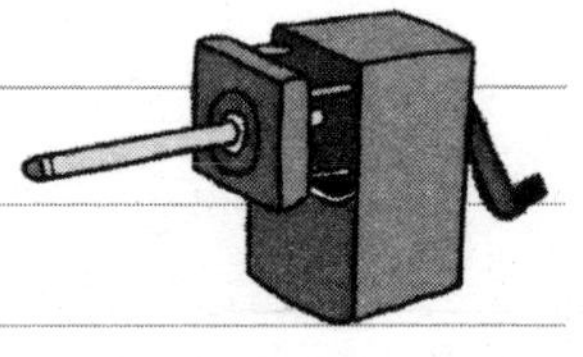

I also heard him ask Miss Nichol if she wanted a cup of tea, and then his hand began to snake towards her mug.

'NO!' she said, slapping her hand on top of it. 'Mine.'

I think he tried to mesmerise her then because he started wiggling his fingers around in the air, but Miss Nichol just said, 'Are you doing a TikTok?' Then went back to her marking.

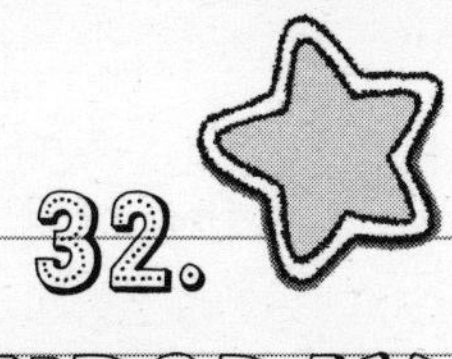

32. THURSDAY

Tomorrow we're doing the assembly and
I STILL DON'T KNOW MY LINES!

I'm going to do a magic spell!

I'm going to do a magic smell!

I've been practising with Stink whispering them from my hair, but because she's under my hat she's hard to hear and I keep getting the words wrong.

Not only that, but the rest of 7N seem to be amazing.

Nelly the Element (Mara) and her gang have worked out an impressive dance routine and everyone seems to know their lines. We still haven't heard Kabir's rap – our rehearsals are too short – but he promised Miss Nichol that it's . . .

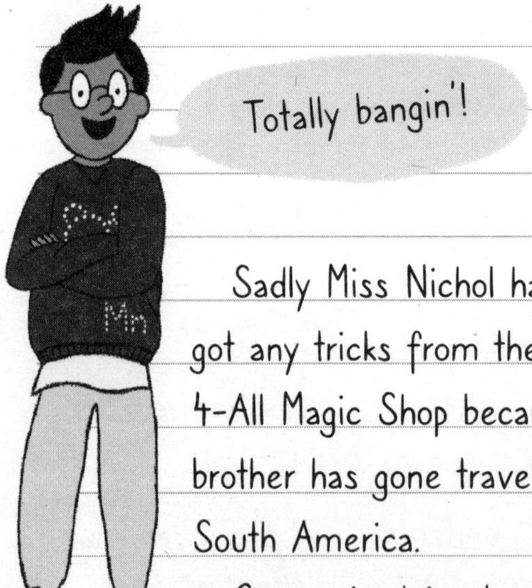

Totally bangin'!

Sadly Miss Nichol hasn't got any tricks from the Trix-4-All Magic Shop because her brother has gone travelling in South America.

Cooper is doing backflips behind Kabir when he raps.

I might be the only bad thing about our assembly.

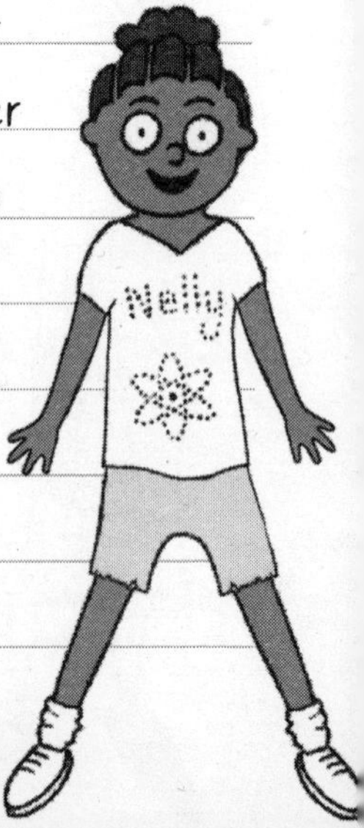

But I'm not giving up. Too much rests on me being a good wizard tomorrow. If I do a good job and Stink gets her wand then I can stop being Disco Danny, get rid of Rufus and Stink will go back to Fairyland all in one go.

It's funny, but now that I've met Rufus, Stink doesn't seem so bad. Today she let Miss Nichol's gerbils escape **AND** dropped a Malteser out of my hair while I was talking to Mara, but at least she isn't planning to take Miss Nichol to Fairyland.

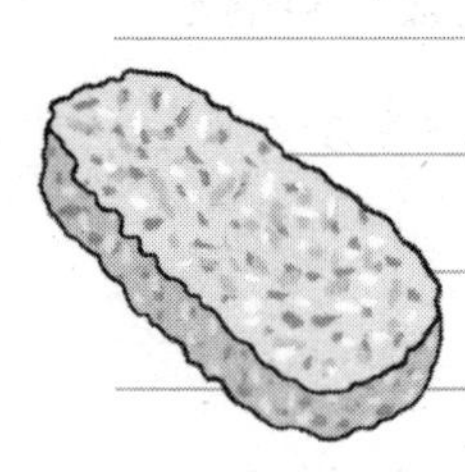

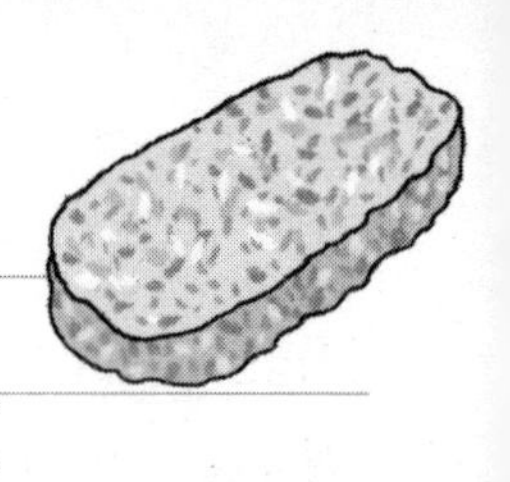

33. SHOW TIME

I set my alarm clock for six, ate a champion's breakfast (three Weetabix covered in Biscoff spread and chopped banana) then got myself in the wizarding zone . . .

I only stopped shouting '**SILENCE!**' when Dad came in and told me he would sell my XBox on Ebay if I didn't shut up.

Stink was still asleep in my rats' cage so I woke her up and asked her to go through my lines with me. She said she was too hungry to do that so I made her some toast. She's eating it really slowly, so it looks like I'm not getting any last-minute practice.

Mum just popped in to tell me that she and Dad are both coming to watch the assembly. GULP. I am starting to feel nervous.

Stink and I are going to school now. Wish me luck!

34. WOW

Wow . . . I mean, WOW! Where do I begin?

I knew I was in trouble before we even got to school because as Kabir, Stink and I were going through the gates, Fandango jumped out of a bush . . .

Fandango, you massive egg weas–
What are you do–
Arghh! What is tha–

That's right: Fandango froze all three of us. While students streamed past us we had no choice but to stand there like statues. We couldn't speak until Fandango unglued our mouths so he could interrogate us. He zipped back and forth in front of our faces yelling stuff like . . .

Does the name Nobeard mean anything to you?

Have you seen this wizard?

If you're telling the truth how come your eyeballs are sweating?

Does this suit go with my eyes? What about my wings?

Yuck. Mum and Dad say you're my sister, but I think they found you in one of those hairy pellets that owls sick up!

Then Stink replied, 'Yeah? Well, I think Mum and Dad found you in a . . . a . . . a . . .'

Stink couldn't finish her burn so Kabir came to her rescue by yelling . . .

WITCH'S ARMPIT!

Unfortunately for Kabir, Mrs Busby was just walking over to find out why we were standing still instead of going into school. Fandango unfroze us then flew into a bush.

Why did you just call me a witch's armpit, Kabir Ullah?

I didn't. I was saying the name of our band.

Mrs Busby narrowed her eyes and said in that case Witch's Armpit could perform at the end-of-term talent show.

Then she let us go so we could get changed into our costumes.

35. NELLY THE ELEMENT AND THE WIZARD OF DOOM

I stood in the wings of the stage holding my foil-covered baguette and wrapped in Scott's dressing gown. Marshmallows kept falling off my beard, but I was too nervous to eat them. My stomach flipped and I needed a wee. Stink helped me calm down by peering round the curtain and giving me a running commentary on what was going on in the hall.

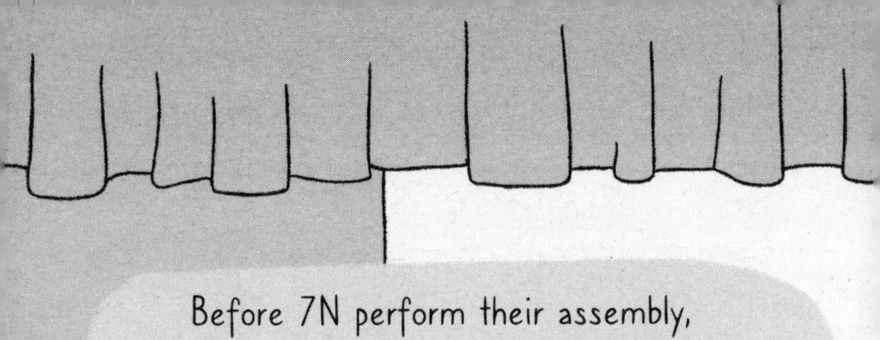
Before 7N perform their assembly, – Nelly the Element and the Wizard of Doom, I have a few notices to read out.

All the Year 7s have come in and the form teachers are here too. SOOOO many people! It looks like the big kids are coming in as well as the prefects. I think that old lady who usually sits outside Spar is here . . . and Kabir's mum . . . and your mum and dad and Sophie. Ha ha! She's dressed as Iron Man. Wow, Danny, the hall is PACKED!

What he didn't know was that my plan was coming together too. All I had to do was walk on the stage and blow the audience away with my performance.

I tightened Scott's dressing-gown belt and rearranged my marshmallow beard. Then I stared straight ahead and held tight to my foil-wrapped baguette.

On the stage, Mrs Busby said, 'I am now going to pass you over to the capable hands of 7N!'

This was it. My big moment. All I had to do was stride on to the stage and say in a booming voice, 'I am the Wizard of Doom and I am looking for that pest, Nelly the Element!'

What could go wrong?

36. DRESSING GOWN DISASTER

I couldn't walk on to the stage. Sweat trickled down my face and into the marshmallows of my beard. For a moment I thought Rufus had done a freezing spell on me, but he was busy rifling through his teabags. He was so confident I was going to muck this up on my own that he hadn't even bothered to do any magic on me.

I was frozen with stage fright!

Stink whispered in my ear. 'Get out there, Danny. I'll help you, I promise. It's my good deed, remember? Now get on that stage and be the best wizard you can be!'

It was a good speech, but I still felt scared. Then two things happened at once.

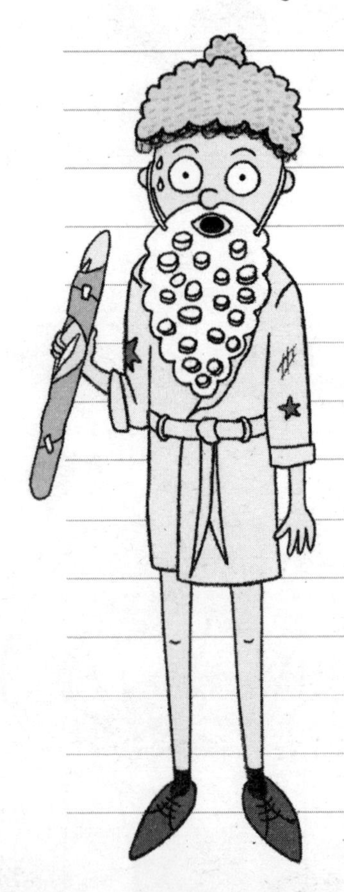

Rufus shoved me on to the stage and Stink shrank down Scott's dressing gown.

I have found out that this was an accident and she was actually trying to **GROW** my beard so it was more impressive, but her broken wand let her down. That's how I ended up going on stage like this . . .

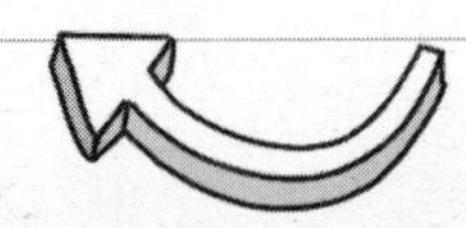

When everyone stopped laughing I cried out in my best booming voice, 'I am Nelly the Pest and I am looking for that dizard Woom the Element!'

Next, Nelly and all her friends burst on to the stage and Kabir did his rap.

He was amazing! I felt a bit guilty as I remembered all the times I'd ignored him over the past couple of weeks.

The audience loved his rap too.

Just then I noticed that Rufus Nobeard had moved round to the other side of the stage and was showing Miss Nichol his box of teabags. His hand moved closer to her mug.

A voice hissed in my ear. '**SAY YOUR LINE, DANNY!**'

I looked up and realised that the audience were sitting in silence, waiting for me to speak.

Stink tried again. 'Danny, say, **OH NO, YOU DON'T!**'

But I didn't say anything, because at that moment a dazzling flash of gold shot through the hall doors and came hurtling towards me.

It was Fandango and he was flying so fast I yelled out and stumbled to the back of the stage. I cowered behind some cardboard rocks. No one else had spotted Fandango, or if they had, they couldn't see him now because he had flown behind the cardboard rocks with me.

Meanwhile, the other students from 7N were giving me furious looks and whispering things like . . .

I wanted to stop hiding behind the rocks, but just as I was grinning nervously and wondering what to do, Fandango did the **RIGIDUM CORPUS** spell on me again.

Now all the audience could see was this . . .

Stink did her best to help. She poked her head out from under the hat and did a reversing spell, but her wand was so battered nothing happened. Meanwhile, Fandango had spotted Rufus Nobeard standing in the wings.

Aha! There is the villain. Now I will destroy him with my most deadly spell: **MORTIFERUM DISSOLVERE!**

But that's the dissolving spell. You can't do that, Fandango. It's **ILLEGAL!**

Shut up, pea-face. What happens in Humanyworld stays in Humanyworld. No one in Fairyland will ever know unless you tell them. Which you won't because if you do, I'll **MORTIFERUM DISSOLVERE** you too!

Fandango was about to do a dissolving spell on Rufus Nobeard and there was nothing I could do to stop him! I couldn't move a muscle. Plus, Rufus was standing next to Miss Nichol. What if she got dissolved too?

Rufus looked up. Perhaps he had read my mind or perhaps he had spotted the gleam of Fandango's golden hair. His eyes fixed on Fandango and he whipped his own wand out.

Fandango snarled. Rufus hissed. Sparks fizzed from their wands.

They looked furious. They looked like they might dissolve the whole school!

'Stink, do something,' I said through clenched teeth. I couldn't move my grinning mouth but I could just about talk.

'I can't do **ANYTHING!**' she cried. 'My wand is totally busted, Danny!'

If only there was someone else who could help, I thought, and then I remembered that the perfect person was standing close by . . .

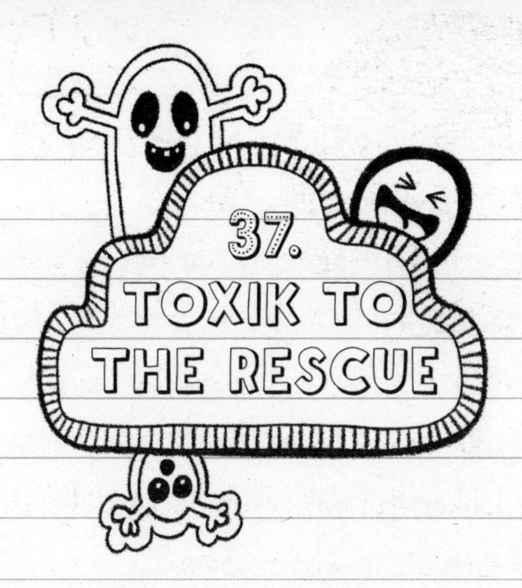

37. TOXIK TO THE RESCUE

Kabir was standing at the front of the stage. He was surrounded by Nelly's gang who were patting him on the back and congratulating him on his rap. A few weeks ago he'd have been checking in with me, making sure I was getting on OK, but it was like he'd forgotten me.

And who could blame him? I'd been a rubbish friend recently. I'd been so embarrassed about being Disco Danny and obsessed with trying to be an amazing Wizard of Doom that I'd barely thought about him.

While I gazed at Kabir, Rufus and Fandango continued to growl at each other and the audience saw this . . .

I had to get a message to Kabir, but I couldn't move and I could only just speak! Then I remembered that I had my very own fairy.

'Stink!' I hissed through my clenched teeth. 'Go to Kabir. Tell him I'm sorry I've been a bad friend and that his rap was amazing. Tell him that I need his help because I can't move and Nobeard and Fandango are about to **BLOW THIS SCHOOL TO BITS WITH MAGIC**. Got it?'

'Got it!' she said, then she flew across the stage.

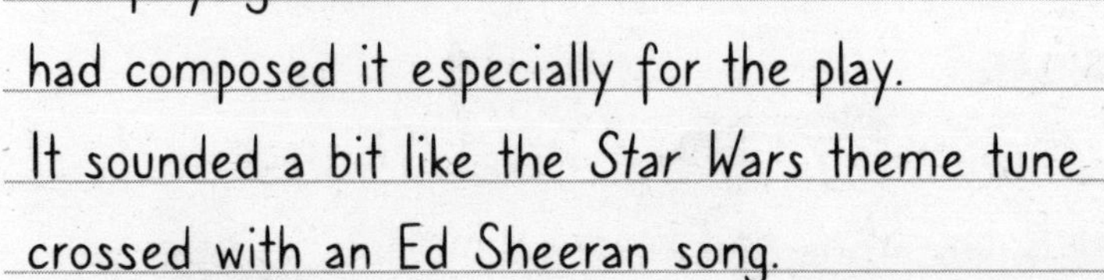

You should know that all the time this was happening music was playing. Scott had composed it especially for the play. It sounded a bit like the *Star Wars* theme tune crossed with an Ed Sheeran song.

Miss Nichol was totally unaware that standing next to her was a wizard who was about to fight a fairy. She just jigged along in time to the music and mouthed, 'Say your line, Danny!'

But of course, I couldn't. Miss Nichol frowned and stepped towards me. Now she was standing right in the line of fire.

I tried to yell: **'GET OUT OF THE WAY! MR NOBEARD HAS A WAND AND IS ABOUT TO USE IT!'**, but because my teeth were stuck together it came out as:

GRR OOO ORF ERR AY! RRR OOEARD AHH A EEER ANG ERS ARAR OO OOZE ERT!

'What?' said Miss Nichol, stepping even closer.

Desperately I looked across the stage at Kabir. Stink had reached him and was whispering in his ear. He frowned. She whispered some more. Then he looked over at me.

HELP ME, KABIR! I pleaded with my eyes.

His eyes flicked from me to Rufus, then to Fandango who was still hiding with me behind the rocks.

Stink flew back to me and burrowed into my hair.

I told him, Danny. I told him everything you said, and a few other things as well.
Ank ooo.

What would I do if I was Kabir? Would I help someone who had been ignoring me for days, or stay where I was, well away from the powerful magic of Rufus Nobeard and Fandango Tink?

Luckily for me, Kabir is a great mate.

He winked at me then ran into the middle of the stage. Now he was standing directly between Nobeard's and Fandango's pointing wands.

Rufus started to dart from side to side, trying to get a clear shot at Fandango, but Kabir moved with him. Rufus was fast, but Kabir was even faster.

The audience gasped and there were some sniggers. I knew why. Kabir looked like he was dancing. He looked a bit like Disco Danny. No, he looked **WORSE** than Disco Danny. He had a look of extreme concentration on his face as he tried to keep up with the swishing wands. Of course, the audience didn't know that he was trying to stop Miss Nichol and me from being dissolved. They thought he was doing the worst dance in the world.

Soon the sniggers became full-on laughs and ToxiK was forgotten as Kabir pumped his arms and wriggled his hips.

Suddenly I felt an explosion in my hair and Stink shot into my lap. Clutched in her hand was a dazzling wand. Stars fizzed from the end of it.

I've done my good deed, Danny!
I've got my Mercorn 1000 wand!

In my muffled voice, I said, 'Why? I've been a rubbish wizard!'

My good deed **WASN'T** helping you become an awesome wizard. It was making sure you and Kabir stayed friends. It's Kabir who makes you stand tall, not wearing a cool cloak or having fire come out of your fingers . . . although obviously those things would help. Especially right now.

I looked up.

Kabir was still throwing himself around on the stage, desperately trying to stop Rufus and Fandango from firing spells at each other. He was doing a great job, but he was starting to look tired.

It was my turn to help him.

'Use your new wand to undo Fandango's spell!' I said to Stink.

'It's a hard spell,' she said, eyeing her new wand. 'But I'll try!'

She pulled back her dazzling wand and yelled, '**SUPROC MUDIGIR!**' A clutch of tiny stars hit me in the chest and the next thing I knew I was leaping out from behind the cardboard rocks.

At the same time, Kabir slipped on a marshmallow that had fallen off my beard and went down hard. Rufus saw his chance and drew back his wand. Fandango shot out from the cardboard rocks yelling, 'I'm going to melt that wizard!'

Finally I had said my line.

The audience stopped laughing at Kabir.

Nelly and her gang and the rest of 7N stared at me in amazement.

I had **NEVER** said my line so well. This was the moment in the play when Nelly was supposed to use kindness and teamwork to defeat my magic, but I couldn't worry about the script now. I had to save Miss Nichol and possibly the whole school.

I didn't have a plan. I just followed Rufus's training and felt the fire of a thousand dragons burning in my core . . . then I unleashed their deadly power.

38. THE FIRE OF A THOUSAND DRAGONS

With a roar, I leaped over Kabir and ran towards Rufus, reaching for his wand. That was when Rufus, Stink and Fandango let their magic fly.

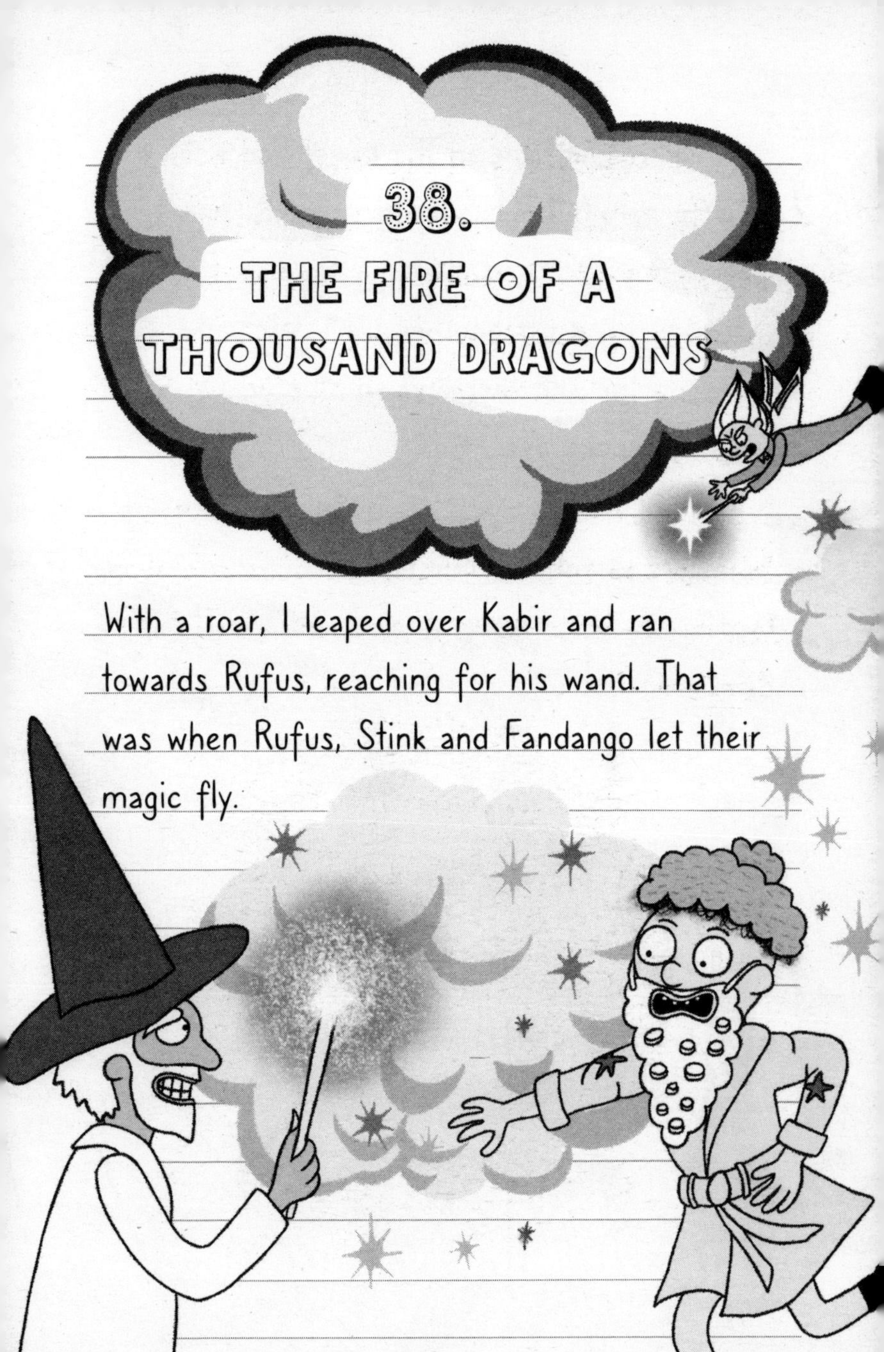

A spell caught me in the chest and sent me spinning across the stage. In seconds, I was back on my feet and charging towards Rufus. Fandango fired off another spell. It caught Rufus on the shoulder and smothered us in a cloud of smoke and stars.

Fandango zipped past my face, wand raised.

'Oh no, you don't!' cried Stink.

Then she managed to grab hold of his foot, yanking him back.

'Let go of me, Sa–'

But Fandango didn't get to say the rest of Stink's name because she went wild.

'**DON'T YOU DARE SAY MY NAME!**' she screamed, then she fired off a volley of spells.

I didn't get to see what happened next because suddenly Rufus loomed out of the smoke and pointed his wand at my chest. This time the spell was so powerful I was blasted through the smoke then rolled backwards off the stage. I lay in a heap on the floor. The hall was in total silence. Then the clapping started. The audience thought this was all part of the show.

Suddenly Stink was back by my side. 'Get up, Danny. Get up!' she hissed. 'Fandango has gone! I burned his wig and that was enough to scare him off, but Rufus is still around. You've got to find him!'

I staggered to my feet and clambered back on to the stage.

The applause got louder. There were whoops and cheers. Dad jumped to his feet, then yelled:

'THAT'S MY SON!'

A chant of '**DANNY! DANNY! DANNY!**' began.

'Quiet! **QUIET!**' cried Mrs Busby, but no one listened to her.

'**DANNY! DANNY! DANNY!**' everyone cried. I didn't hear a single Disco Danny.

The smoke cleared. Miss Nichol was coughing and spluttering. Rufus reached for her mug.

'Let him have it, Stink,' I said.

As I grabbed my foil-covered baguette off the floor and pointed it at Rufus, Stink did another spell with her Mercorn 1000. Perhaps she wasn't aware of her new wand's mighty power. Perhaps she just did a really good spell. All I know is **THIS** happened . . .

When the smoke cleared I saw that Rufus had shrunk to the size of a mouse. I rushed forward, scooped him up and popped him in the pocket of Scott's dressing gown.

'Where did you learn to do all those stunts, Danny?' asked Miss Nichol. She looked dazed and confused, but she was still clutching her mug.

'I've been practising at home,' I said. 'Did you like it?'

She grinned. 'I **LOVED** it. I knew you'd make a great wizard.' Then, as the audience clapped and cheered, she looked around and said, 'Where has Mr Nobeard gone?'

TOXIK AND THE WIZARD OF DOOM

See what I mean? **WOW!** What a day!

The rest of the day went by in a daze. Possibly because I was high on my success in the assembly, or possibly because I had got a bit of concussion when I rolled off the stage.

Who knows. What I do know is that not a single person called me Disco Danny.

I don't think I'd have cared if they did.

At lunchtime I hung out with Kabir, Cooper and Mara in our form room. The now tiny Rufus Nobeard was shut in my lunchbox and Stink was in Miss Nichol's cupboard trying out her new wand. Every now and then a puff of smoke or a star escaped, but no one noticed. We were too busy reliving our triumphant assembly. Miss Nichol was right. It was epic, and so was being with my friends.

Mara even shared her Scotch egg with me.

After school Kabir, Stink and I went straight back to my house. It was time for Rufus to go back to Fairyland.

We tied him up with Sophie's scrunchies then got ready to push him back through the door. I asked Stink if she wanted to take him herself.

'Imagine Fandango's face if you were the one to hand Rufus Nobeard over to the FBI,' I said.

'Nah, I don't want to do that,' said Stink. 'The worst thing Rufus ever did was kick those mermaids out of their castle, and **THEY** had stolen it from a gang of rude princesses.'

'Plus, there's that thing you told me, Stink,' said Kabir. 'You know, when Danny was stuck behind those cardboard rocks.'

'What was that?' I said.

Stink shrugged. 'Just that I wished I'd been a better mate to Rufus. If I had then maybe he wouldn't have become wicked.'

'That's true . . .' squeaked Rufus.

I'm sorry, Rufus. I shouldn't have abandoned you. How about next time I'm in Fairyland we go out for a unicorn milkshake or something?

'Maybe . . .' said Rufus.

He was trying to act all casual, but we all saw the smile tugging at the corners of his mouth. And it wasn't a wicked smile. It was a happy one.

In the end we took off the scrunchies and Rufus walked through the fairy door on his own. He wasn't entirely good as he left. Before Stink shut the door he shouted, 'This isn't the last you've heard from me, Daniel Todd! I'm going to come back and –!'

But we didn't hear any more because before he could finish his sentence, Stink gave him a push and slammed the door shut.

40. SAUSAGES AND JELLY

Once Rufus was gone, Stink entertained me, Sophie and Kabir by showing us some of the spells she could do with her new wand. She turned water into bubble tea, gave Tony and Noah the power of speech for a few minutes and made one of my pointy shoes float.

I want a hat made of cheese.
Yesterday I ate the rubber off a pencil.

Then she started doing jelly jinxes and sausage hexes. Soon I had two chatty sausage rats running around and half the things in my bedroom were encased in jelly.

Humans smell like carrots!

Stink looked up at me. 'Do you want me to go now, Danny? I did say that I'd go away and leave you alone once I'd earned my one hundred nuggets . . . but I could help you and Kabir rehearse for Witch's Armpit.'

When Danny's asleep Stink lets us out of the cage and I lick Danny's face!

'What's Witch's Armpit?' I said.

'Our band,' Kabir reminded me.

PLEEEEASE let me stay, Danny.

She made her eyes go **VERY** big.

So did Kabir and Sophie.

Don't send Stink away, Danny!
Yeah, everything's better when she's around!

Was it? It was certainly stickier, and messier, and funnier . . .

Stink's eyes went even bigger.

'Perhaps you can stay for the weekend,' I said.

FART
THANK YOU, DANNY TODD, BEST HUMAN BEING EVER! THANK YOU!

That all happened a few hours ago. Right now Stink is chilling out with the rats in their hammock and I'm writing this wearing Scott's dressing gown. It's grown back to its normal size and it fits me perfectly.

Tomorrow Stink and I are meeting up with Kabir so we can buy sweets. We're planning to hang out all day in Najin's garden. We might write songs for Witch's Armpit, or we might go out on the SUP board.

When we're at the shops, if someone shouts, 'Oi, Disco Danny!' or dances in my face, I know I can handle it because I'll have two friends by my side. Well, one of them will be by my side, the other one will be in my hair. I might even do the dance right back at them.

But for now, this is Disco Danny and his fairy, Stink, signing out.

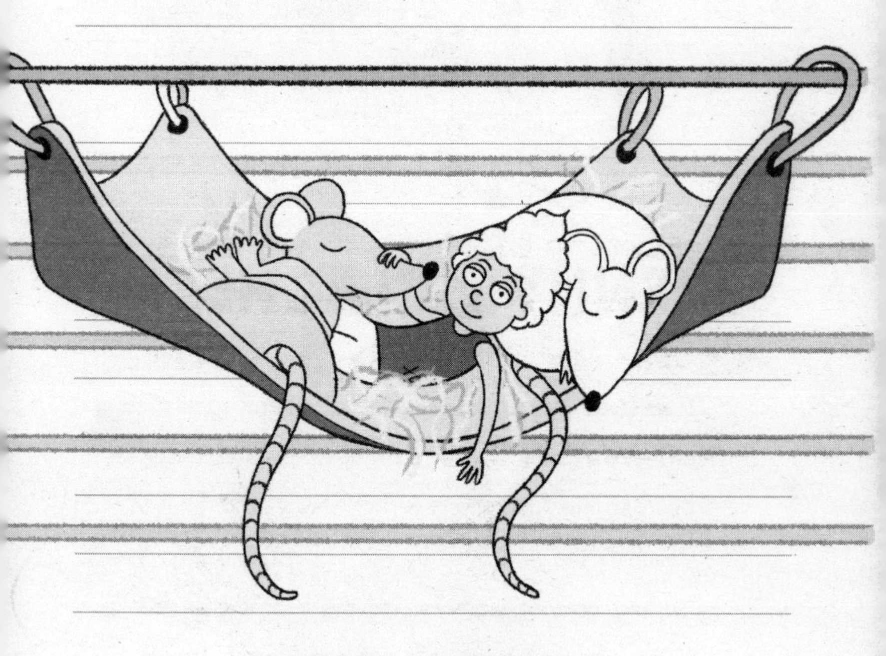

THE END

JENNY MCLACHLAN

is the author of the bestselling Roar series and *Dead Good Detectives*, as well as several acclaimed teen novels. Stink is her first author-illustrated series. Before Jenny became a writer she was an English teacher; she now lives by the seaside and enjoys writing, drawing pictures, and daydreaming on the South Downs with her dog, Maggie.